Sweet One

CRISTIN HARBER

BOOKS BY CRISTIN HARBER

THE TITAN SERIES:

Book 1: Winters Heat (Colby Winters)

Book 1.5: Sweet Girl (Prequel to Garrison's Creed)

Book 2: Garrison's Creed (Cash Garrison)

Book 3: Westin's Chase (Jared Westin)

Book 4: Gambled (Brock Gamble)

Book 5: Chased (Asher McIntyre)

Book 6: Savage Secrets (Rocco Savage)

Book 7: Hart Attack (Roman Hart)

Book 8: Black Dawn (Parker Black)

Book 8.5: Live Wire (Jared & Sugar Westin)

Book 9: Bishop's Queen (Bishop O'Kane)

Book 10: Locke and Key (Locke Oliver)

THE DELTA SERIES:

Book 1: Delta: Retribution

Book 2: Delta: Revenge

Book 3: Delta: Rescue

Delta novella in Liliana Hart's MacKenzie Family Collection

Each Titan and Delta book can be read as a standalone (except for Sweet Girl), but readers will likely best enjoy the series in order. The Only series must be read in order.

Sweet One

CHAPTER 1

GOD. **IF NICOLA COULD SUCK** on any more ginger without *that* making her want to puke, she would. But for the time being, it was about the only thing that was keeping her from hugging the bathroom toilet. The nausea would be over in a few weeks, and Beth had promised her that morning sickness was a blessing anyway. She said it meant everything was ticking along as it was supposed to—though Beth was her best friend and a spy, not an obstetrician.

Ugh. Nicola reached for the remote as her phone rang and flashed the word UNAVAILABLE. It was way too early for Cash to check in from his job. A different kind of stomachache set in. "Hello?"

"Nic?"

"Parker." She sighed, relieved. If something were wrong, Jared or Roman would call. "What's up?"

"Are you okay?" he asked.

"Yeah. What's up?"

"Baby's doing okay?"

"Yes, Parker." Trepidation began to tickle her tummy. "What's going on?"

"Anyone there with you?"

"Oh, shit. Parker. What is going on?"

"You have to talk to Roman."

Her stomach bottomed out at the mention of her brother. "Is he okay?"

"Yes."

"Is Cash?" Her world went into a tailspin. A cold shiver slid down her spine, and the hair on her arms vibrated in fear.

"He needs you to talk to him."

"He *who*?"

"Both of them. Sit down, sweetheart. I'm patching you through." Parker was too serious, and an eternity of stress aged Nicola by decades as he cleared his throat. "Mia and Sugar are already on their way to your place."

Tears burned Nicola's eyes; anger at the unknown made her grind her molars. "Damn it, Parker. What's happening?"

A jarring noise broke in with the loud beat that could only be the inside of a helicopter. "Is Princess on the line?" Jared's low voice scratched through the line, breaking in and out.

"Yeah, Boss," Parker said.

"What the hell is going on?" she asked. The urge to

vomit tested her limits, and not knowing what the hell was happening was too much to take. "Parker? Jared? Who the hell is on the line?"

"Nicola," her brother interrupted. "Nic—"

"Roman? Where's Cash?"

"Nic—"

"No, no, no. Where's Cash? Tell me! Where's Cash?" Her world spun. Tears rolled down her face as she fell to her knees. Everyone was on the phone except for her husband. He didn't know she was pregnant. She'd wanted to surprise him, to shout, *You're going to be a daddy!* and see his beautiful tan face light up and those perfect dancing blue eyes shine with the brilliance that she'd remember forever.

"He's fine." That was a lie. She'd known for years how Roman sounded when he wanted to protect her and make everything alright, as a big brother should. "It'll be okay. Just listen to me."

Shaking her head, she curled onto the floor, silent tears soaking her skin and desperate exasperation making her hyperventilate. "What is going on, Roman?"

"Calm down, sweetheart."

"Roman! Don't you dare tell me—"

"I know you're pregnant."

"Oh God! No!" If he knew that, then Beth had told Roman, and Cash was in bad shape, and this—Roman calling her—was the last straw: an attempt to save her husband or a good-bye call. Her mind spiraled.

Screw the silent tears. Nicola sobbed. "Where's Cash?"

"He's with me." Roman's stoic voice faltered, telling her all she needed to know. "He's sleeping, hon, and he needs to hear your voice."

"Oh God." She wiped her face, unable to see past the blinding tears. "Roman, no. Please."

"He's okay, Nic. And he's going to be better when he hears your voice." Roman paused, and Nicola shook, not sure she had the strength Cash needed. "You've got to do this for him. Got me?"

God. Everything about their lives was always torn apart. She couldn't lose him again. Nicola wrapped her arms around her belly. She wasn't showing, but in there was their baby—a tiny little bit of him and her—and they were going to be Mommy and Daddy. Cash had no choice but to survive whatever had happened.

The tears paused. He wasn't leaving her. Nic searched for the right words. Nothing came out. She cleared her throat. "Put the headset on him, and get off this channel."

She was going to order, beg, plead, pray, push, and do whatever the hell it took to have Cash stay on the phone with her until it was safe. She remembered the night he spent on the phone with her when she was in Istanbul and the day they were on the phone and his truck blew up. This was their thing. Long talks on the phone meant survival. She wouldn't lose her family— any of them, actually. "Wait. Roman?"

"Yeah?"

"You're okay?" If her big brother hadn't mentioned he was hurt because Cash was hurt worse, then she had words for him too. "Everyone else is okay?"

"Yeah."

"Good." Nicola squeezed her eyes shut, focusing her fight. "Please. Don't let me lose him."

"Give me a three count, and he's all yours. You talk to him until we land. Three…"

CHAPTER 2

"CASH." NICOLA COULD WHISPER, OR she could yell. It didn't matter—that much she knew. "Just you and me on a headset. Almost like old times."

Nothing.

She'd expected him to respond, maybe remember that time when they were flirting with the idea of getting back together. She'd been in Istanbul and Cash stateside, and he'd talked her through a worrisome night while a contract killer slept only a hotel room away.

"Roman says you're hurt. Jared doesn't pull punches. If you weren't in a bad place, he wouldn't do this—have me talk to you. And, yeah, Parker asked me to have a seat. That's Parker for you: always with the risk analysis. God forbid he tell me something awful and I pass out, hit the floor or something…" Pain sliced her throat as she rambled. "So you're not doing too well, huh, honey?" Tears streamed down her face. "But here's the thing. I need you to come home."

Silence.

"*We* need you to come home."

Nothing.

"You're going to be a daddy, Cash."

Nicola let the words hang in the air. "So many things to say." She sniffed. "And I can't find the words for any of it. All the things… I don't know why I didn't tell you at first that I was pregnant, that you were going to be a dad and I was going to be a mom…maybe I wanted to find the perfect moment. Maybe I was meant to save it for this. Maybe you can hear me, and everything happens for a reason—" Her voice cracked. "And this, our, baby, she's, he's going to *save you*. Bring you back home to us." Fat tears streamed down her face. "Please, please, *please*, Cash. Please. You can do this."

Her breaths shook, and she let unbridled terror reverberate through her limbs. As the shakiness ended, Nicola dropped to the floor, holding the phone to her ear, limp and lost, crying and missing his arms around her. "Don't die on me."

There was so much silence except for the distant whisper of background noise.

"Don't you dare die on me. I love you too much to let you go. Don't you know that? Didn't I tell you that after you were hurt the last time?" When he and Roman had been hit by an RPG in that armored SUV, he'd sustained a head injury—a brain trauma. The doctors said he had to take it easy, and he'd tried, staying off the job as much as a man like him could.

"God," she prayed for the both of them. "Whatever it takes. Whatever is wrong with him this time..." She never should have let him go out on a job again after his somewhat recent history of accidents and unconsciousness. One trauma in such a short time period was not good; a couple was awful. In her spiraling mind, injury upon injury meant compounded bad news.

"Cash! You are not blowing yourself up anymore! You have a baby to come home to! You have *me*." She sobbed, lost all over again. The tears came and came and wouldn't stop.

The line beeped. "Nicola, it's Parker."

Wiping her eyes. "Yeah?"

"They're ten minutes out. Brock said whatever you're saying is doing something. Okay?"

"Okay." She bit her lip, terrified to hang on to that twinge of hope.

"He's a fighter. You know that."

She pushed the tear-soaked strands of hair off her face. "Yeah."

"Nicola?"

"Yeah?"

"I'm jumping off this line, but you've got this. He needs you. Okay?"

"Yeah." It was the only thing her numb mind could think to say.

Another beep, and Parker was gone. She was left with silence. She wanted Cash to smile through the line and say, "Hey, sweet girl."

"You said we'd spend the rest of our lives together. It's not done. We're not done! We have too much left to do. A baby. *Babies*. We've yet to jump out of a helicopter together." She laughed quietly even through the tears. "I don't know about you, but that's a bucket-list item. What else? God. We have so much, too much, left to do."

She ticked the items on her fingers as though he could see her, imagining that maybe in his muteness, he was making his own list as well.

"You're going to have to change a diaper. I'm going to have to figure out how to outshoot you at the GUNS. We need to run that obstacle course together over at HQ. You know the part that shoots mud balls and swings live wires? And I'll try my hardest to beat you. It won't happen, but it will be so much fun."

She paused, desperately wanting to hear him laugh.

"When we cross the finish line—no, right before we do—I'll speed up, and you won't slow down, and I swear, I will *almost* take you. But I can't beat you. I know that. You know that. The only time I'll ever admit it is when you're unconscious." Her voice broke. "But you'll grab me, swing me around, and kiss me."

When was the last time he'd kissed her—right before he left? They were running around, rushing. Surely he'd kissed her good-bye. But she couldn't remember. Shit. She couldn't remember the last time his lips were on hers? God, no…

Trying to stop the new onslaught of tears, she wiped haphazardly at her cheeks with the back of her hand, faking encouragement in her voice. "No matter that I'm sweat drenched and panting like a crazy woman. You'd kiss me because you love me almost as much as I love you—*Please*." The tears came fast and furious. "Life's too much fun with you. You're my person. My man. My hubby. And a daddy."

Silence.

"You all are landing soon, and I'm coming to find you, but when I do, you better be awake. Okay?"

Like he could say a word, when that's all I want him to do.

"I'm going to take that as a yes."

And if she never heard *sweet girl* from his lips again, she might just die alongside him too. "Cash, baby, I love you too much. It's not time to let go yet."

Dead air.

In the distance, someone knocked at her door, but she couldn't move.

"Please. Please. Please," she whispered.

The line beeped. "Nicola, it's Parker again. They're dropping in on the chopper pad. Grab your go-bag. We'll get you over there ASAP."

Sugar and Mia walked in. Leave it to Sugar to bypass Nicola's security system and break in when she was having a life crisis.

"Are you okay?" Mia mouthed.

Nicola shook her head.

"We'll be in the kitchen," Mia said, but neither she nor Sugar moved.

"Okay, sounds like the girls are there," Parker said almost reverently. "Stay on the line another few seconds. He's at Landstahl, and the doc will call you soon as there's something to say."

"I don't want to get off the phone." More tears leaked.

Mia put her hands on Nicola's shoulders. "It will be okay, Nic."

"They have to get him off that chopper," Parker said. "Headset can't stay on forever."

"I know." She sniffed, wiping unsuccessfully at her cheeks. "But I can't."

"They're going to disconnect."

"You have to do it, Parker. I can't."

"Ten-four, sweetheart."

Five minutes later, the line died. Nicola crumbled. She was already on the floor, a bawling mess. But this was something else. The phone fell from her fingertips, slipping to the carpet. Mia's footsteps came from the kitchen, and she dropped next to her, followed by the click-clack of Sugar's heels.

"Okay." Sugar crouched down too. "So first we stop for a drink. Then we get on the jet."

So no one knew she was pregnant. She sniffled, too exhausted to begin that conversation.

Mia's face pinched. "Or not."

Nic glanced from one woman to the next. Maybe they did know.

"Like a drink of—" Sugar's face twisted as she obviously tried to come up with something appropriate. "Milk?"

Okay. Nicola couldn't help but smile. They were confirming without asking. They knew without her having to tell them. "Sounds great."

Sugar lifted her shoulders. "So booze and caffeine are out?"

Nic nodded.

"Congratulations, then?" Sugar asked.

"Thanks," Nicola whispered.

Mia hugged her. "Congrats. It will be okay."

"Get your bag," Sugar ordered. "Do you need to go puke or something? I guess you don't have"—she used air quotes—"the *flu* anymore. How does that work? Morning time only or what?"

"Pretty much all the time."

"Glad we drove in your car." Sugar raised her brow

to Mia. "Shotgun." Then she looked at Nicola. "Unless the front seat means you don't puke as much."

Only Sugar. Nicola rolled her eyes. "I can keep a lid on it."

"Good. Keep it together until we're where we need to go." Assessing Nicola in a way that only she could do, Sugar clapped her hands and pushed off the ground. "I might call an audible, but for now, I'm riding shotgun."

Mia stood and pulled Nicola up. Side by side, Mia and Sugar were comical. Mia wore a very cute, super-soft sweater. She could have walked off the front pages of any number of department-store catalogs. Sugar was all in black except for a magenta XOXO written across her T-shirt. They were an unstoppable force hell-bent on saving her and Cash.

Nicola hugged Mia all the time, mostly because Mia was huggable and liked hugs. Sugar, on the other hand, wasn't and didn't. Nicola didn't care. She hugged the snot out of Sugar, making her squeak.

"What are we doing?"

"It's a hug, Sugar. Shut up."

"I *know* it's a hug."

Nicola didn't let go; she and Sugar had way too much history not to hug at a moment like this. "Ask Jared for practice. You suck at it."

"Oh, for crap's sake." Sugar made a huge show of throwing her arms around Nicola too. "I love you, girl. Nothing's going to happen to our boy. Okay?"

Nic nodded into Sugar's hug. "Okay."

"Don't get your tears or snot on my shirt. The only ones allowed to do that are your future children."

Nic laughed, breaking the strong hold on Sugar. "Alright."

"Ready?" Mia asked.

Nicola inhaled a slow breath, for a second believing that everything would be okay. Simple hugs—that was all they were, but they were soul repairing. That was the power of friendship. She had her tribe, and they gave her the strength she needed to take that step forward. "Let's go wake my husband up."

"Such a lazy ass," Sugar mumbled.

"Jeez, Sugar," Mia whispered. "Tone it down."

"Please don't." Nicola walked to get her go-bag. "If anyone is not themselves, I might really start freaking out. So Sugar needs to stay an insensitive bitch."

Sugar beamed. Mia shook her head, and Nicola dug through her bag, ditching anything that might be used on an actual job and replacing it with prenatal vitamins and enough ginger to stock a sushi shop. "Let's do this."

CHAPTER 3

THERE WAS NOTHING MORE TERRIFYING than the man in the white coat. Surrounded by the hum of fluorescent lights in the quiet conference room, Nicola sat across from the brain-trauma specialist who had overseen Cash's care since he had arrived. She simply stared as the doctor organized a folder on the table that most likely contained charts or concrete data for an uncertain prognosis.

"When will he wake up?"

Dr. Lobani smoothed the edge of the page. Nic's fingers fluttered in her lap. She and the doctor had similar tics. His wasn't necessarily the nervous energy that hers was, but nonetheless, he didn't stop moving.

"It's not that easy. Cash sustained—"

"I understand what he went through." She'd forced Roman to give her every single gory detail. "I want to know two things. One, he obviously is past the point where he will die on me, right?"

"At this point, your husband is stable."

Her fingers fidgeted as she ignored his generic answer. "And two, when will he wake up?"

"I can't give you that answer."

"Does he just open his eyes and—what, we start therapy? He's going to be groggy? What? I'd like some details here because—"

"Because you're overwhelmed and feeling the timeline of your pregnancy."

Her shoulders slumped. Saying it like that made her sound selfish. But it was also true. "I want my husband healthy and at home, yes."

Dr. Lobani leaned back in his chair, tapping his fingertips together before steepling them. "Most coma patients wake within days."

Days! That didn't sound too bad. She had thought weeks; in the made-for-TV movie about their lives, he would wake up to find his kid in college or something.

"They don't just suddenly arise, but rather, it's a waking process. Moments of alertness. Passing realizations coupled with long bouts of rest."

"How long?"

"Gradually. He'll stay awake with us longer, and we can assess how he is."

"Meaning?"

"We'll determine what steps he will have to take in recovery."

That made sense. It wasn't as if her husband would just wake and skip out of the hospital, one hundred percent better. What if he didn't wake? "Do stable patients always get better?"

"Our focus is Cash. Not patients in general. Let's watch his progress over the next few days."

"But that does happen? Sometimes stable people don't wake up?"

He shook his head. "Brain injuries manifest in many ways. We need to watch your husband, and prepare for future rehabilitation."

"What kind of things"—Nicola cleared her voice, trying to hide the fear—"should I be prepared for?"

"It is a wait-and-see situation. The brain could—"

She flattened her hands on the table. "What kind of things?" She hoped he'd see past the shock and anger and understand the level of desperation that she was teetering on and her need to plan for the future. "Please."

"Anything from a lack of motor skills, mental reasoning, and verbal abilities to cognitive deficiencies."

"Meaning what? Cognitive deficiencies?"

Again, the doctor scrutinized her, likely knowing that she was Titan and former CIA and that if she wanted to, she'd torture the information out of him. But his eyes showed compassion and acknowledgement that they were just two young parents, wanting desperately to live their lives together. "Concentration, memory, speed of processing information. Things of that nature."

Cash's career would be over if he lost all of those things. She gulped away the hurt that she prayed he would never know. "That's all, huh?"

"Impulsiveness, confusion."

"That was sarcasm, Doc."

Dr. Lobani rubbed his forehead. "There's no need to worry about what may not be an issue."

"He's had brain trauma before."

Nodding, he said, "I've read his file."

"Not good, right?"

"Many circumstances can affect TBI."

"What's that?" she asked.

"Traumatic Brain Injury."

Was that a label that a parent-to-be was able to handle? Nicola fidgeted. "What am I supposed to do?"

"I wish I had a better answer."

She looked at the doctor with raised brows and an unsteady gaze. "Than...?"

"Wait and see."

ONE NIGHT AND TWO DAYS later, the vigil hadn't

changed, and the doctors weren't making Nicola feel any better. Even the nurses were giving her pitying looks.

Exhausted didn't begin to describe the toll her body had taken, and she tried to hide it from the world—from herself—mostly because the medical center's OB-GYN said the baby was fine, and that was all that mattered. And if the baby was okay, everyone could stop bothering her.

The door pushed open, and Nicola turned to see a man she didn't know.

"Hello, sorry to interrupt. Don't mind me. I'm upgrading the software on a monitor."

Nic smiled. "Sure." It wasn't the first time that someone had tromped into Cash's room. The guy was in uniform but wasn't medical personnel, and he looked miserable. "Are you okay?"

"Sure." He squinted. "Do I know you?"

She shook her head. Even on a secure base, she was paranoid. Having a history in witness protection, the CIA, and Titan would do that to a girl. "I don't think so."

His eyes flashed to where names were normally listed on the wall for patients, but because of the classified relationship that Titan had with Landstahl, Cash Garrison was simply listed as "Patient, Room 6806."

After an awkward pause, the tech tinkered with a

machine. It beeped a few times as he reset it, then he turned, staring. They were about the same age, and he searched her face as though he had a question.

"Do you need something else?"

"No, ma'am." He looked away, clearing the inquisitive expression from his face, and scurried out the door.

Nicola's gaze narrowed on the empty space where he had been. She was always on red alert. Was it safe to bring a baby into their world? Sure. Mia and Colby had kids. Sugar and Jared. Brock and Sarah. They had intense safety-and-security protocols, some of which bordered on paranoia, but Nicola appreciated them. She settled down, telling her hormones to take it easy. No sense in riling herself up when she couldn't do jack about it.

Sugar's heels clicked down the hall, announcing her arrival before she walked in. Nicola wiped under her eyes, knowing full well that she couldn't swipe away dark circles and bags. She shifted from her chair by Cash's bedside as Sugar walked in.

Her dark eyes looked from Cash, in the same state he'd been in for two days, to Nicola, in the same place Sugar had left her. "You look like crap."

"Jeez, sunshine. Thanks for coming over."

Sugar extended the coffee cup in her hand. "Decaf tea."

Nic nodded. "Thanks."

"You need to eat."

"I did."

"When?" Sugar snapped the word in what was probably meant to be uber-caring but to the outside world likely looked scary-slash-bitchy.

Well...good question.

"That took way too long to answer." A couple click-clacks of her super-high-heeled boots, and Sugar was next to Cash, inspecting him as though she could see something the doctors couldn't. "He's not going to wake up in the next fifteen minutes. You need to eat."

"I have breakfast bars."

"You need to eat, Nic."

"I'm not leaving him."

"For Christ's sake, Nicola." Sugar tossed her bright-red-fingertipped hands in the air. "He'd kick my ass for letting you and baby just sit here, crunching on protein bars. If you don't come with me, you'll have an entire contingent of dudes to deal with."

Nicola blinked. "Excuse me?"

"None of them know how to deal with a pregnant superspy. But what they do know is that if you don't take care of yourself, they will force you to do it. For you and for him. For that little tater tot growing inside you."

She smiled. "I think it's more the size of a blueberry right now."

Sugar grinned too. "I missed that part of the moms' club. It was a guess."

Jared and Sugar's daughter, Asal, was adopted, and Nicola wondered how deep Sugar's maternal clock ran, but now wasn't the time to ask. "I don't want to leave him, Sugar."

"You're scared. I get it."

She dropped her head. Being scared wasn't something that any of them ever talked about. Fear was part of the job. They accepted it and moved forward. That was why they were excellent in their roles with Titan and their partners—Sugar, Mia, Sarah, and even Beth to a certain extent because she and Roman had something long-term happening. But there was another level of fear that they had to live with in addition to what they might encounter on a job: what if the job was too hard? What if a spouse was hurt? What if they said good-bye to their spouses for the last time?

Nicola's throat tightened, and tears stung her eyes. How much more could she cry?

"Nope. No more tears right now. Cash, man, I'm taking your woman for some hot grub in the cafeteria. Don't die while we're gone."

"Christ, Sugar," boomed a voice from behind Nicola. Jared walked in. "Take it down a notch already."

"Hey." Nicola lifted her chin to say hello.

"Hey, Princess." He pulled a chair and gathered

Sugar onto one knee, where the ballsy, brash woman compliantly perched then eased. They were two harsh people, but when coupled, they were soft and in love, although with an I-can-kill-you edge.

Her stomach growled. It was all the talk of food. She certainly was taking very good care of herself and the baby, eating lots of calories, protein, and carbohydrates—everything that their bodies needed. Nicola had even double-checked with the doctors that the stress wasn't causing undue stress to the fetus, and they'd had her examined by an OB. Maybe she was hungry. But she didn't want to leave Cash. It was that simple.

"Nicola," Jared said.

She tore her attention away from Cash, not realizing that she'd been lost—again—in his face. Scratched and bruised, he rested quietly just as though he were sleeping the day away. "Yes."

"Go with Sugar. Get some grub. A change of scenery. It's an order, Princess."

She dropped her head, not wanting to say no to Boss Man, but—

"And before you fight me on this…"

Nic lifted her eyes.

"Roman's bugging out of his fuckin' mind. If nothing else, give him five minutes. Go talk to him."

She dropped her head and rubbed her temples. Roman always took care of her, and she'd forgotten to even have a conversation with him. "Yeah. Okay."

"With the exception of when he's checked on you two, Roman hasn't moved." Sugar stood. "I'll show you where he's posted up. He's pretty much just stood there, waiting for you."

Nic's heart clutched. She had a good brother, a good man, a good team, and good people all around her. If Cash didn't make it out of this, they'd still be okay. Her eyes burned, and a sear of pain ran down her throat.

"Up and out of the room," Sugar said. "You're crying away all of your calories. I'm pretty sure you need those to build body parts."

Jared smacked her butt as he left. "Let me know if she gets out of line."

Sugar smirked. "You know I mean well."

Nicola smiled limply. "I'd worry if you were polite or appropriate." Then she leaned over Cash and brushed his hair with her hands, letting her fingertips drift over his stubbled cheeks. "I'll be back soon. I love you." Nicola kissed his lips, lingering and scared to leave.

"Nic, he's going to be okay."

She squeezed her eyes shut, kissed him one more time—hating how his lips didn't feel as though he were *just* sleeping—and followed Sugar numbly out the door. Sugar hooked an arm around her shoulders, dragging her out of the room. As they walked down the hall, the normalcy with which people seemed to live their lives struck Nicola as absurd.

"Food, then Roman."

Nicola leaned into Sugar, needing her hug more than she realized. "Good plan."

Five minutes later, Nic had a tray of bland food, but despite being hungry, she wanted none of it. Sugar was as bossy as Boss Man, though, so filling her tray with a couple of muffins and a bland chicken sandwich passed muster.

Sugar bagged her food at the to-go counter, and with stern orders to eat, dropped Nicola off where Roman and Jared were poring over files in a meeting room. Jared cracked his knuckles as he stood, nodding to both of them, before leaving with his wife.

"You doing okay?" Roman asked before wrapping her in a bear hug.

"You've already asked me that."

He squeezed her before releasing. "You keep lying to me."

She laughed quietly. "Guess that's what I do."

He closed his eyes and snagged her in another hug. "Nic."

Somewhere in that hug, she dropped the to-go bag, and then she lost it, shedding all the pent-up tears. So many times she'd lied to her brother: when they were teens and she should have told him that she was in love with his best friend, when she should have called him while she was in witness protection even though she wasn't allowed, and when she'd let other people tell him he was going to be an uncle.

Roman gave bear hugs. The good thing about a brother who was as broad and tall as the hospital they were in was that he could easily lift her up and relocate a heaving, sobbing, hysterical woman without a blink of effort.

"Breathe, Nic." He rifled through her bag of food and brought out a stack of napkins then offered one for her tears.

"God. I'm such a freaking mess."

"You're going through a lot." His elbows were on his knees, and he leaned forward, brows pulled down as if he were trying to read her mind.

"You're going to be an uncle."

Roman leaned back an inch, a tiny smile on his face. "I know. Congratulations."

She sobbed.

"Damn, those pregnancy hormones aren't anything to mess with."

Nic reached out to smack his arm, but he grabbed her and hugged her again. "Seriously, Nic. Congrats. You guys are gonna make killer parents. Mom and Dad are gonna freak out, and everything is going to be fine."

"I have secrets all the time. There's something wrong with me. I'm going to be an awful mommy." She bawled. "I kept secrets from you back in the day. How'd that work out? Bad. Then from Cash? Same thing. And again from Cash? He doesn't know. He. Doesn't. Know!"

"Take a breath. It's not the same thing."

"I'm so screwed up."

"You're not," he said. "Why didn't you tell him the second you knew?"

She wiped her face. "Because I wanted to plan a surprise. Something special. When he was off job. Not with just a day off but, like, a couple weeks."

"See? You had a reason."

"A lot of good that did me."

She dropped her head. "He might die not knowing."

"He won't. He's going to live because of that pregnancy."

Surprise stopped the tears. "What?"

"I told him."

"What?" Her eyes went wide. "When?"

"Right after the attack, when he was first hit, I needed something to keep him here with us—even if he wasn't waking up. So I told him." He shook his head. "I'm sorry. I know that's yours to tell him. But I..." Roman stopped and rubbed his face. "He needed to hear it. Even if he didn't know he heard it."

Nicola launched into her brother's arms. "Thank you."

"A lot of hugging today."

"You're a good hugger."

"I know."

"Cocky too."

He laughed. "I know."

"I told him too." She pulled back and grabbed the bag of food, suddenly finding the urge to eat a muffin. "I think it helps."

Roman nodded. "All the medicine in the world? That baby is what's bringing our boy home."

"Yeah."

They sat in silence as she finished the muffin and gauged her need to puke. It wasn't there. That was progress. "So… Beth."

Her brother's eyebrows went up, and he smiled. "Beth."

"About damn time."

"Agree." Roman nodded, saying all they needed to say. The tension between the two had been noticeable to the entire team, but neither Beth nor Roman had outwardly admitted any interest.

Nicola was happy for them, but it only reminded her how much she needed Cash. "I'm going to go back to my husband. I need a nap."

Roman gathered up the papers that he and Jared had been working on. "I'm out too."

"Take care of Beth, okay? She fights you because she needs you. When that last mental hang-up of hers is gone, she's yours forever."

"*I* know that. When she clues in, what is supposed to happen will happen."

God, her brother was the right guy for Beth. "Right answer."

"Glad you think so."

"I love you, Roman."

"Love you too, kid. Go take care of our boy. And my—niece? Nephew?"

"Too early still." Nicola's stomach fluttered as she wondered if Cash would want a boy or girl.

"Alright. Either way, go." Roman turned her out the door and sent her packing.

A minute later, she was looking at Cash's hospital bed. Nothing else mattered but her family. She dropped the bag, slipped off her shoes, and crawled in next to him, snuggling under the covers and hating every second he didn't call her "sweet girl" and kiss her goodnight as she drifted to sleep. Memories of sleeping together under the stars on their first date, and how magical that was, replaced her worries about the stiff, silent man next to her.

CHAPTER 4

BILLY TWAY CHEWED THE INSIDE of his mouth, backing out of the door, trying not to trip over his feet as his mind raced. He somehow knew what he'd seen on the other side of that hospital room door was his ticket out of hell.

"Hey, Twat Waffle," a uniformed Army a-hole joked as he passed.

"*Tway*," Billy said, the response he'd given more often than any other in all his years in the military. Maybe more than "Yes, sir." Everyone liked someone to pick on, and Billy had been the guy.

"You missed a spot." The jerk—from the back of his head, he looked to be an eighteen-year-old ground pounder—never slowed down.

"I'm not the janitor!" *No one* respected him! Even the newbies. Billy couldn't control it. Both hands went into overdrive, punching middle fingers into the air.

The kid laughed. "Easy, broke dick."

But he never turned around. "What the fuck? What the fuck?" Billy wanted to charge and jump the man from behind but needed to concentrate on what he'd just seen in the hospital room. His mind was all over the place.

Bouncing in place, his torn mind had problems deciding which direction to take. Go after the young one who needed to know what his last name really was, or follow up on the thought tickling the edge of his mind?

The newbie looked over his shoulder before rounding a corner of a hallway. His face was pure, antagonizing bait. Billy took the bait and swallowed it—and charged.

An unseen arm jutted out. The blunt obstacle from out of nowhere caught him like a concrete clothesline, and he went down, coughing and sputtering. A med tech who had tried semisuccessfully to watch his back over the years shook his head, looking annoyed. "Cut the shit, Tway."

Tway. Billy's throat might've been crushed, but he could breathe better at the sound of his last name. Not fucking *Twat Waffle.*

"You stand no chance with anyone on base."

"Not true." He sputtered.

"Keep your head low, and you're out of here. Fuck up, and you're in the brig. What don't you get about that?"

Billy pushed onto his butt, sliding against the wall. "We had a situation."

The med tech shook his head. "Keep your head low. Try to stay out of trouble, and you get to go home. Don't you get it? *Don't fuck up.*"

Billy pushed off the ground. "All day long, all I do is *fix* fuckups."

"I'm doing you a favor. Guys like you need 'em. Read me?" With a pitying shake of his head, he started walking away. "Go to your bunker. I'd stay there."

Billy hadn't had a single friend, not one companion through the hell of boot camp and orders. Even though he was less than twenty sleeps from a ticket the hell home, barely anyone knew his name. Over the years, his med-tech *friend* had claimed he wanted to keep him out of trouble. What about the assholes who spent their time picking on Billy? Was there a poster for orientation that introduced him as the onsite entertainment? No one would miss him when he was gone—though they'd miss him fixing all their fuckups.

How could an entire medical facility be inept enough to break their computer systems on almost a daily basis? How could they have so little respect for the *only* man who could fix their screwups? Doctors might save lives, but not if they couldn't order and review the simplest of medical reports and see MRI results.

Like the one that was done in Room 6806. That woman.

Billy's mind processed information almost as quickly as Landstahl's servers. In an instant, he knew that innocent face that peered up at him—although it was exhausted and older than the last time he'd seen it, which was in pictures from the news in Podunk, Virginia years ago. Nothing ever happened in his hometown, so when the story had hit, it hit big.

Billy knew that woman's story just as well as he knew all of his true-crimes TV trivia. He might've even had a crush on her. It was weird to think of a dead woman as attractive, but she was, and this many years later, her face had stuck with him. Now he knew why. What he didn't know was how she was *alive* and sitting pretty in a room reserved for military special guests.

Could it be possible that two people from a small town in the US would find themselves in a hospital facility in Germany more than a decade later? Not likely. But stranger things happened. People hit the lotto. Hopeless illnesses were cured.

No, he was smart, but he was also stressed. Maybe it was time for those pills that the doctor had offered to help calm him down. Billy hadn't wanted anything to cloud his mind, to slow his fingers on the keyboard. Those pills would make his fingertips shake, according to everything he'd ever read on the Internet. Plus, they'd dull the acumen that kept him sharp when name-callers who wanted to see him fail surrounded him.

At a computer near the nurses' station, Billy pulled

the records for Room 6806 under the guise of doing a system upgrade. He'd land himself in a FUBAR world of hurt if he was caught snooping records—especially in public—but he couldn't help himself.

Even as he typed, scouring for the name of the woman in Room 6806, he knew the answer: Nicola Hart—the same college kid who died in a car crash years ago. Half of the Gianori mob had gone to jail because of what the FBI had found.

But what if none of it were true, and she hadn't died? *Conspiracy theory much?*

Room 6806 was inaccessible. Yes. Huge conspiracy theories. *Holy crap.*

It was time to go back to his office in the underground lair where they hid the IT geniuses who kept this place running. There he could dig, see what there was to see, maybe watch some Netflix on lunch—a good mobster documentary or two—and if that was Nicola Hart…then he had a meal ticket.

The military wouldn't hook him up with a shiny new job when he was back on US soil in less than a month, and Billy wasn't re-upping his contract. He had no jobs lined up and zero prospects, a small pension, and less in his bank account—*thank you online gaming.* But Nicola Hart's existence was the kind of information that the Gianori crime family would feast on.

Or rather, *pay* on.

CHAPTER 5

NOTHING WAS BETTER THAN A dream about a hug from a man who couldn't hug her. Nicola woke nestled in Cash's arm. The only upside of this trip was it had scared the morning sickness out of her.

She sighed, burrowing into him, hating the shitty hospital mattress and plastic-foam pillows, but at least Cash was warm albeit unresponsive. His heavy arm draped over her acted as a security blanket, and even though she positioned it as if he were an inanimate object—almost having to growl at some of the nurses to stay away—it made her feel better.

"Morning, Cash." She tilted to kiss his very scratchy cheek. Maybe it would be a good day to trim that beard. "It's also a good day to wake up."

No response—as usual.

She snuggled back in, loving the quiet moments before the doctors and nurses, Roman and the guys, and the entire world arrived to show support and give them strength. "I love when it's just the three of us."

Cash squeezed her gently. So nice—wait! She jumped up in bed. "Cash?"

Nothing.

Straddling him, she put both hands on his chest and willed him to move or even blink. "Cash?"

"Easy, cowgirl."

Nicola jumped. *Sugar.* "I didn't hear you come in."

"That's because you were manhandling your husband."

"God." She climbed off the bed, running her hand over her face and into her hair, wanting to rip it out in frustration. "He moved."

"Didn't they say it would happen?"

"But I was talking to him, and he, like...responded." *To talk about our family.* "You know what? He needs to come home. He needs out of this hospital and to have his normal stuff. Like his hat. Where's his hat?"

"He's in bed."

"It should at least be in the room."

Sugar bit her lip then nodded. "Jared can find it. Or Roman."

"And I want to take him home," Nicola said.

Sugar's eyes went wide, and Nic spun toward Cash. His head pushed back, almost as if he were stretching without using his arms.

"Talk about home. I'll go…find someone."

It didn't matter who Sugar would find or how stunned she sounded. Nicola pounced on the bed. "Are you going to wake up?" she whispered. "Because that would be super cool if you did."

He wasn't moving again—back to the relaxed state of nothingness that was Cash.

"We're going to have a baby." She curled back into his arms, wrapping his hug around her. "A little bitty family."

It was a quiet lullaby, soothing her to sleep and letting that dream of his hug come and take her away. Minutes ticked by, and her eyelids felt heavy. She wanted to stay awake…

"Nic." The raspy, gravelly sound whispered in her dream, just loud enough to pull her awake.

She blinked, not believing because as her eyes opened, his body was just the same—unmoving in the silence. Just a sleeping Cash. So handsome, so perfect. "I love you too much; you know that." Her eyes sank shut as her heart and mind warred over whether or not to lose hope. "But I wouldn't change it for the world."

Scooting up, she kissed his soft lips, and—she felt movement. His lips didn't part, but they didn't stay the same. Nicola reared back and stared, scrutinizing. "You're waking up."

Nothing.

She cupped his face. "*Please*. Wake up."

As staring contests went, this one would kill her. It lasted minutes or hours, and he was the most beautiful and heartbreaking thing she'd ever watched.

Her thumbs swept over his cheeks, ignoring the occasional nurse who wandered in. "Today, baby. You're coming back to us today."

His eyelashes fluttered.

God, yes. They did, and he would.

"See, there you go." She curled in close. "You said my name earlier. I know it."

But when she touched his hair and cheeks and the outline of his lips with her fingertip, nothing changed.

A knock at the door pulled her attention, and regretfully, Nicola looked up. Beth and Roman hovered close together with an unmistakable new-couple glow, fingers touching then quickly dropping and eyes locked a few seconds too long before they said their hellos. They looked happy and in love but as if they were trying to hide it lest Nicola have some pregnant-woman meltdown. "I'm fine. Chill out."

"Thank God." Beth bounded toward the bed, Cash's cowboy hat in hand. "You're looking for this?"

"Yes." It was one piece of the puzzle. For ten minutes, they shot the shit, and then Roman and Beth escaped, *holding hands*. Clearly, they were now *publicly* a couple. That was good—Nicola wanted them together almost more than anything else.

Though not as much as Cash waking up. "Get up

already!" She stomped over toward him, put the hat on his head, and glared. Pregnancy hormones were making her Mood-Swing McGee, but all Nicola knew was that at the moment, she wanted to shake him awake.

Instead, she gave him a hug. Then bit his shoulder. Hard.

Cash groaned. His shoulder jumped. His hand moved as though he wanted to brush her away, and Nicola smiled in triumph, kissing where she'd almost drawn blood. "That got your attention, didn't it?"

His eyelashes fluttered, and Nicola watched as the most beautiful blue eyes that she missed more than she could believe stared back at her.

"Hi." The word barely choked past her lips.

He didn't respond and drifted back to sleep. A total letdown.

Then his shoulders bunched. His eyelashes fluttered again. Hesitantly, Cash's eyes opened, and he looked around the room. He didn't show any recognition, but he didn't seem uninterested either. So that was okay? Her worry spiked.

"You were hurt, but it's okay now," she said, hoping to soothe him as much as her.

He focused back on her. His tongue darted out and licked his lips. With a jerky switch, he shifted, and his cowboy hat fell over his face. Nicola grabbed it, noticing that he didn't react.

"So…" She should call the doctor or page the nurse,

but they said he'd wake up, and that it wouldn't be a ten-alarm fire when he did. She wanted to take it slow, just as they'd advised, and give him a moment before she pressed the call button.

His eyes stayed glued to hers.

"You can hear me?"

His lips twitched, then a smile flickered before it stayed. *God.* There was that Cash Garrison lazy-boy grin before it gently faded.

"Good. You have this IV, and you're peeing in a bag. All things super awesome." She laughed, hoping to make him smile again, but his intensity scared her. "Do you know who I am, Cash?"

His head tilted in a slight nod.

"God. Thank God." Nicola launched into his arms. He barely moved, and she didn't care. She took hold of his arms and wrapped them around her. "Oh, thank you, thank you, thank you."

Practically in his lap, she pulled back, half-praying, half-ready to kiss the ever-loving snot out of him. "If you know who I am, say my name."

Cash rolled his bottom lip into his mouth. His eyes bounced from her to the wall, the IV, and back again, and with it went her stomach and her hopes. All her fears came back.

His chest expanded as he drew in a breath, and she watched, waiting, knowing it would be a slow road, knowing she needed to chill. She wanted to tell him it was okay, that he shouldn't rush. The words would come, and he wasn't scampering to get away from the crazy woman crawling all over him. So it was all good.

Nicola dropped her inquisition and laid her head on his chest then propped her chin to stare up at him, still with his arms manhandled around her.

Cash licked his lips again, his face drawn as though he were almost pained. "Sweet girl."

Then he gave her his perfect smile and, slow seconds later, that Cash Garrison wink.

That was all it took. All the tears that she'd had before came back, but this time, it was complete, consuming, absolute rejoicing. "Yes, I'm your sweet girl."

CHAPTER 6

"I'M HOLDING YOUR HAND." NICOLA held tight, and Cash's heart squeezed as hard as his hand did.

So did his frustration. What a fucking double-edged sword. He could literally feel how much she loved him, but at the same time, he was crawling out of his skin in a need to be normal again. He had a shit-ton to say, but there were moments his lips took an extra second to form the words.

How did that make him one of the world's best snipers? It didn't. In what way was he the best of the best when it came to special ops now? There was just no way.

And how could Nicola look at him as an equal partner—in marriage, at Titan, in life? His stomach turned, and he wanted to vomit. *Fuck.* Or really, he wanted to get his ass down to a firing range and blow something up. Blow *everything* up. He was angry in a violent, raging, out-of-character way.

She leaned into him but didn't let him take her weight. That he had to think about lifting his arm and pulling her in was a problem, but he did it anyway.

"I like being tucked under your arm," she whispered as they walked toward the medical center's conference room.

"I hate..." *That you narrate everything...that I can't find the words to say this...that it's all stuck in my brain.* "You're talking to me like a kid."

"Doc said to say everything."

He kissed the top of her head. "Always the good student." He opened the door, and they were the first ones in the little room. It was cold, and the table sat eight. His operative training should've kicked in to assess the scene in a blink of an eye, but he found that he counted the chairs. *Fuck.* Then he lifted his gaze to check for the entry and exit points. Vents, lights. Where should he sit? Where should Nicola sit? Everything was always strategic. But for the moment...he plopped into a seat.

"Doing okay?" she asked.

Cash forced a smile, and hers registered that she knew his grin was fake.

Dr. Lobani came in. They did the handshake thing, everything uncomfortably forced and awkward as though Cash was readying for a death sentence.

"So let's hear it. What do I need to know? If you

could hit me with bullet points, cut the—" His mind stuttered for too long a second. "BS. I'd like that."

The doctor agreed. "You tell me when you have questions."

They nodded.

"Closed-head injuries like yours, due to the combination of explosive blast waves, concussive forces, and blunt-object impact, create contusions. Or rather, bruises in the brain. You're lucky that there were no skull fractures, no hematoma—"

"Thank God," Nicola murmured and squeezed his hand. They'd both read up on what went down when Cash had been injured.

"No two brain injuries are ever alike, meaning that no two recoveries are ever alike. The most important part of treatment..." Dr. Lobani narrowed his gaze on Cash, and he knew a bombshell was coming. "You must relax and give yourself time to heal."

"I can relax," Cash grumbled, and that was a lie. Or at least, he couldn't relax in the way that a brain-trauma specialist would approve.

"Relaxing might mean different things to us." The doctor knew this game well, Cash could tell. "Until you're fully recovered, you'll have a range of effects: headaches, mood swings, irritability, ringing in your ears. Stay away from percussive forces. For example, no rock concerts. *No time on the range.*"

"I'm a sniper. That's how I chill."

The doctor gave them both a pointed yet sympathetic stare. "Exercise falls into the category of *not right now*. As does any vigorous action, including some sexual activities."

As Cash shifted in his seat, *that* caught him off guard, and he wasn't sure how or why taking his wife had to do with healing his brain, but he wasn't going to ask a follow-up—

"Until when?" But apparently Nicola *was*.

"A few weeks downtime, followed by playing it by ear," Dr. Lobani said plainly as though reporting the weather prediction. "I'd suggest holding off."

"Right," Cash grumbled. "And getting back to the fact that I'm a sniper, I need time on the range." And *vigorous activity* with his woman would happen when they wanted…

"I understand your concerns, and I deal with your type. So I'm going to lay it out there so you understand this in no uncertain terms." Dr. Lobani leaned forward, clearly familiar with hard-asses. "If you want to continue as a sniper ever again, you have to take care of yourself *now*."

Ever again. Acid bit the back of Cash's throat. "Right. Okay."

"No caffeine. No alcohol. Your body needs time to find its baseline, and stimulants slow the process."

"Easy. That's fine." Cash shrugged. "Nicola's on a decaf kick; I can be too."

Nic coughed.

"You okay?" Cash asked.

"Yup."

He turned his attention back to the doctor. "No drinking. No shooting for a limited amount of time."

"For however long it takes. And we need to get you in to see a vision specialist. Ophthalmology will see you today and—"

"I'm sorry, what?" Panic. That was panic. Brain bruises were one thing. No beer—that was another. But his vision? That was his meal ticket.

"Traumatic brain injuries, what we call TBI, directly affect vision. We need to see how it's affected your sight."

His chest puffed out. "*It hasn't.*"

"And we'll know when we have the exam. Balance is also a concern. We have—"

"Nothing has changed." If it had, his career was over. The bile at the back of his throat climbed higher. His hands clammed up, and Nicola's grip tightened until he realized he was hanging on to her with everything he had. "My eyesight is perfect. Give me a week or two, and I'll belly-crawl a tightrope."

Dr. Lobani nodded. "To ensure that, let's stay on the safe side for now. No high visual stimulus: no TV, limit your cell-phone usage unless you need to make the call, and don't stare at the screen. No tablets, no movie theaters."

"Well, jeez, Doc. What is it that you suggest I do?"

"Relax with your wife. Take a vacation before—"

Nicola sputtered into a coughing fit. "I'm fine, I'm fine. Sorry. We can do that."

The doctor nodded. "Go lie on a beach."

Peachy...from action hero to a lump of nothing in the sand.

"WHAT AREN'T YOU TELLING ME?" He tugged her closer. It was enough to feel like a damn invalid, shuffling around the hospital, having his wife treat him with kid gloves, having the entire damn team act as though his mind would turn to mush if he so much as sneezed, but there was more, and he was done with the dance.

"Nothing."

"Bullshit, Nic." They pushed into the cafeteria. "Everyone's got an eye on me."

"You're lucky to be alive."

They grabbed two chairs and settled down. "Are you hungry?"

Her face twisted. "No. But you have to be. What do you want? I'll get it."

"Nic. Sit."

She flitted and doted to the point where she might

as well have donned nurses' scrubs. "Seriously. I'm going to take care of you."

"Sit down, Nicola."

"Cash—"

"I can get my food. I can get yours. Nothing like that is going to change because I was hit on the damn head. Christ."

Toying with the edge of her shirt, she shrugged. "Honestly, I'm not hungry. I was just trying to help."

"I get the recovery thing. But I'm not helpless." Everyone acting as if he was a wounded warrior when there were actual wounded warriors in this place was driving him mad.

"I know."

"And there's something everyone's not telling me."

Her eyes shifted.

"Damn it." He groaned. "If they're benching me indefinitely—man." Cash pushed out of his chair. "Fuck this. I'm going to find Jared."

"Wait."

He turned toward the cafeteria's exit sign. "His ass is around here somewhere."

"Cash, hold on."

Between the nonstop post-freakin'-coma headache and dealing with this shit, his head was going to explode. The pounding at his temples was literally jumping. If Nicola looked closely enough, she could probably see his veins bulging. She snagged his hand, easily catching up because, damn it, he couldn't escape nearly as fast as he needed to.

"Wait."

"No." He brushed her off. "The conversation needs to be had."

Nicola pulled him hard, tugging him through a door that led to an outside garden. The cool air slowed him down and forced him to take a break, but it would only last for a shock of a second. His little thing of a wife was able to push him around. Thank you, damn TBI. This shit was going to drive him insane. However fast they said he'd rebound, it wasn't going to be fast enough.

Cash put his hands on her shoulders. "Good looking out, but I'm going to talk to him."

"That's not it." Her deep-chocolate eyes were wide, almost scared, but something more. Excited? Fearful? His brain couldn't connect the dots to figure out what.

Nicola put her palms on his stomach and ran them up his chest, encircling his neck, and hugging him.

"Fuck, Nic. You're starting to scare me." *What am I missing?* He wondered if he had amnesia. Maybe he was off Titan. Maybe he'd dreamt the whole thing about marrying Nicola. Maybe his life sucked, and it wasn't this grand, perfect thing that he'd forced himself to wake up for.

She put her chin on his sternum and stared up,

blond hair framing the face that he'd crawled through the darkness to come back to. "Don't be scared."

"Nicola?"

"I'm pregnant. We're having a baby."

Shivers ran down his neck and spine. He blew out a breath as tears stung his eyes. "You're pregnant, sweet girl?"

She nodded into his chest, her eyes glistening.

"Oh my God."

"You had to come home to us." Her whispers ended with tears. "And you did."

His mind couldn't find the words, but his body responded, and he engulfed her as completely as he could. The hug held the sentiment. He buried his lips into her hair. A tear escaped, then another, and he breathed her in, knowing that everything in the entire world had just changed.

They clung in love, in tears, in relief, together, forever, before he took a deep breath. "You're okay? Everything's...okay?"

She nodded. "I'm not very far along, but yeah."

"Good."

Her smile beamed as her eyebrow went up. "You're going to be a *daddy*."

"Wow." Just...holy shit. There were no words. "And that's what everyone knows?"

"Yeah. Sorry. It wasn't supposed to happen like that."

He laughed. "I'm sure concussive waves and comas threw off your big announcement plans."

"Yes!" She smiled and snuggled into him. "Exactly."

"So what now?"

"Now I think we talk about your rehab. I'm off job. You're off job."

Cash grumbled.

Nicola rolled her eyes. "Yeah, yeah. So here's an idea. What if…?"

"I'm going to hate it, aren't I?"

"Maybe." She smiled and bounced on her toes. "But don't say no at first."

"No way!"

Nic smacked his chest. "Cash!"

"Easy! They said to avoid reinjury."

"Lord. Glad you didn't lose your humor."

He took her hand, threading fingers with hers. "Tell me."

"There's a great place. It's cute, quiet—"

"Totally my kind of place." He smirked.

"Jared has a beach house in South Carolina. It's near a good rehab place, and there's a great OB nearby. Let's go to the beach."

He couldn't get back on the job. His mind was ten shades of fuzzy, and his muscles took more than a lazy-man's second to do as ordered, and his wife wanted to relax by the beach. It fit with the doctor's orders—lie low, sleep as much as possible—but damn if it didn't feel as though someone was reaching over to take back his warrior card.

This wasn't living at the beach the way a SEAL might train for the battle zone. His career teetered, the idea of the beach house strangling him and shifting him one step closer to a forced retirement. But Nicola batted those beautiful eyelashes, and his mind couldn't process the words needed to debate her.

He stepped closer, terrified of too many things: that nothing would readjust back to normal, that she would see him as damaged, that this grinding self-doubt— feelings he had *never* had an inkling of before— wouldn't dissipate. "Just for a few months."

"Promise!" Nicola bounced onto her toes and kissed him.

His soul sighed. That—this—her. She was what he needed. If his mind couldn't keep up, his body didn't care, and kissing her was easier than breathing. Cash gripped Nicola to him, craving more than those stupid little hi-how-are-you kisses she'd peppered him with in the hospital.

His tongue slid across the seam of her lips, and her instant bounce of excitement melted against him. "Sweet girl."

She nodded, apparently needing this as much as he wanted to taste her. Fuck it. Who cared if there were cameras in the courtyard? She opened her mouth, and his tongue touched hers.

Nicola ran her hands to his cheeks and into his hair, tightening her fingers, tugging at the strands, forcing him to kiss her harder. His chest tightened, and his head went dizzy—not in a TBI kind of way but because Nicola was his drug, and it'd been way too long since he'd had a hit.

Cash pulled back. They needed to get the hell out of the hospital. Jesus. His erection would split his pants if he didn't pull back. She clung to him, her eyes praying for more, her lips parted and panting.

"Cash Garrison."

He raised an eyebrow and tilted his chin up, not sure he had the voice to say anything but *I love you.*

"You kiss like a god."

"I love you." Why even hold it back? "The beach house it is. You and me and nothing to do but each other."

Her lust-drunk eyes went wide, her lips parted farther, and she nodded slightly.

"I can't wait."

CHAPTER 7

"TWAT WAFFLE." MICHAEL MACKEREL, THE junior IT analyst behind Billy, clapped. "Throw me that pen, would you?"

"It's literally two feet away, and *you* can't call me that." The rest of those morons who couldn't find a reset button to save their medical-degreed lives apparently *could* call him that. But a fellow IT guy, newbie, and soon-to-be replacement? He couldn't.

Mackerel laughed. "Right on, brother. Get your briefs in a bunch. Do what you're good at."

"Screw it." Bill had no less than seven more Gianori documentaries to watch, and even with earbuds in, Mackerel was going to cramp his learning curve. "I'll have my pager on me."

"Fight the good fight." He chuckled then whispered, "Twat Waffle."

"God!" Billy slammed his work papers down and

rushed him, both hands out, grabbing a shirt. He just couldn't take it anymore. He was going postal. If only they'd given him a goddamn weapon. But they hadn't. So he bit into Mackerel's shoulder.

Slam.

Billy went up. Then down. His head spun. Everything went dark, then he saw stars.

"Shit," he moaned, grabbing for his head. *God.* He touched his back. Everything hurt.

Mackerel laughed. "Dude. How'd you even make it in this place?"

Billy rolled over, seventy-five percent sure he'd bruised the backside of a kidney, and coughed. "Asshole."

All Billy wanted was to get free of his commitment to Uncle Sam. He pushed off the ground, snagged his laptop to the sound of Mackerel's laughter, and rushed out. Billy had banked documentation and had spent the last day spying on Room 6806. He had enough information to fire off a communication to the Gianori mob.

Not that he was initially sure how to do that. He thought about leaving a cryptic message on Facebook, a vague blog post, or a comment on an Instagram pic. Surely, one of the Gianoris had an email address, but it was likely monitored. Billy needed to be stealthy and think like a criminal. Maybe they'd pay him for his research or offer him a job. No, that was thinking too big, too…corporate.

But people like the Gianori clan, according to everything he'd seen in twenty-two hours of documentary video, paid their informants well. Billy could finally have cash and respect. Maybe the Gianoris could kill off his urge to go postal in this hospital. Selling what he knew about Nicola Hart would actually save lives.

For the first time, Billy had something to look forward to. He hugged his laptop to his chest and skipped to a private conference room, barely ignoring someone who called out, "Watch out, there's a twat waffle crossing.

CHAPTER 8

BILLY PASSED THE ROOM OF Nicola Hart *Garrison*—otherwise known as his meal ticket—twice before he had the nerve to set up another "accidental" meeting. Learning her new last name had been harder than expected. He'd had to tap into medical files, bypassing several layers of security that his employer had in place, and only by chance stumbled upon a *Garrison, C.* on the corner of an MRI in a classified, unnamed medical folder. Someone had fucked up, and that was a big win for Billy. *Thank you very much.* He leaned into the room and—

Empty. No strewn clothes, no sign of a woman living next to her husband in a hospital bed.

"Shit." Billy ground his molars and rolled a pen between his fingers in his pocket. Why hadn't he hurried up his investigation instead of watching hours upon hours of investigative reporting into the Gianori mob?

He paced the small space, letting the fresh fumes of bleach abrade his nose. No one had ever accused him of being a great reporter...but if he wanted to play Sherlock, what would he do next?

First, find Nicola Hart Garrison.

His shoes squeaked as he power-walked down the halls, almost ignoring the trail of *Twat Waffle*s that followed him. All his life, people had made fun of him. Joining the Army hadn't helped. The assholes. All he'd done was join a crew where the bullies congregated. Well, he wouldn't be living much longer among the morons.

He squeaked around another corner and descended the stairs into IT's basement lair, passing the cool kids' front offices and proceeding to the back dungeon, where he was supposed to just work on fixing mindless programs. But now he had free rein to Google *Nicola Hart Garrison*.

He found nothing under that name, so he tried Nicola Hart.

A slew of mob articles and obituaries dating from years ago, and a few descriptions of real-life TV movies that looked to be real tearjerkers popped on his screen. Little did they know *she was still alive*!

Nicola Garrison was his next search term, and again, he found nothing. He typed in "C. Garrison." And that was interesting. The Titan Group. Billy clicked onto their website.

64

Titan Group is a contract-based private security firm with superior security and technology consultants. It provides confidential for-hire assistance, ranging from paramilitary operations to law enforcement to hostage negotiation to rescue operations. Titan specializes in unstable conflicts. It is a privately held company.

Well, damn. He tingled all over, knowing that he stood on the edge of his mobster payout and post-military retirement plan. Hell, call it his post-fuck-the-military plan. This was better than going postal if whatever dots he could connect were actually worth the effort.

Billy clicked on Clients from the drop-down menu. The list made his eyes go money-bags wide: CIA, DIA, MI6, NSA, and on and on...

Over the next five minutes, Billy fell down the rabbit hole that was the Internet, searching all things Titan Group. Finally, he took a deep breath and entered one more search term: Gianori Lawyer. Billy had a deal to make with the devil, and since they likely didn't list their contact info in the Yellow Pages, their lawyer would be the next best thing.

ALFIE ACCARDI STARED AT THE desk phone in his

expensive Boston office, waiting for the Feds to bum-rush the expensive door separating him from the rest of his law firm. Time ticked.

No Feds. No callbacks from what had to be the biggest goddamn moron Alfie had ever spoken to. But...he tapped his fingers on the edge of the lacquered desk. The moron had interesting things to say, things the Gianori would pay to know.

Which was exactly what Billy the Moron had implied. If that was even his real name—given how ridiculously stupid the phone call had been, Alfie would bet money that the man's name really was Billy Tway.

Acting on the information wasn't the issue. The question wasn't whether to act but how. The Gianoris paid him handsomely to protect their interests. A key witness in Emilio Gianori's prosecution a little more than ten or twelve years ago—that was big news. Acting on it would be bigger.

He rubbed his smooth cheeks and contemplated how, or *if*, the exchange of information and payout should be handled. Billy the Moron had tipped his hand and basically given all of his information while Alfie had remained quiet. The ignoramus couldn't stop talking.

At this point, it might be best to let him continue to dig his own grave. The Gianoris had complete deniability, and Billy was hungry to prove himself—a military man of some nature. *He* could do the dirty work; it sounded as though he already wanted to anyway.

"Eh..." Alfie debated the thought aloud. But the mob loved their revenge. Junior would want his chance at Nicola Hart Garrison, who was alive and well and married. He punched the intercom for his assistant. "Vicky, get Junior lined up for lunch at Vito's today."

If nothing else, they'd get a piece of cheesecake, drink a little espresso, and talk about where to hide a body. Like old times. It'd been too long since they'd had one of these chats. Or they could do the practical thing and outsource the job. Time was money...maybe there was a variation that Junior might want to discuss.

Alfie tapped on his desk again, spun the gold cufflink on his shirt before shaking out his sleeve, and punched the intercom for Vicky. "Get me everything you know on Billy Tway. Family. Friends. Military. Rank. Discharge. Where does a grunt like him find a fuck and who would attend his funeral?"

CHAPTER 9

EVEN FOR SUMMER, THE WEATHER was colder than Billy had expected for Boston. He was free. No military code. No army assholes. No orders. No "Twat Waffle." He could go where he wanted and do what he needed, which at the moment was wait for a phone call that his gut said would come. Today was the day.

Until he heard from the lawyer, he'd need to live off the dollar menu at any burger joint he could find. Savings and his pension wouldn't land him on a private island. Gianori money would.

As he was ordering a burger and small fries, his phone rang. He took a seat and—yes! This was the call. He cleared his throat, aiming to look serious and deadly, but he got a weird look from a kid sitting nearby who would clearly grow up to call others names like Twat Waffle.

"Jerk," Billy mouthed before saying, "Hello?"

"We spoke before." The caller's opening was less a hello and more a reminder.

"Yes, sir."

"You check out," the Gianori lawyer said.

Of course Billy did. "As does my information."

An uneasy pause hung on the phone line. "Easy on the phone lines, son."

"Right, right," Billy mumbled. That was stupid. Get it together. "Would you like to meet in person? I can come to your office. I passed it—"

"You're in Boston?" the lawyer asked, and Billy wasn't sure by his tone of voice that the man was as impressed as he would have liked.

"Of course. I'm ready to—"

"Go to Vito's on—"

"I know where it is." Enough documentaries had detailed the Gianori's hangouts. Billy had found the location online and then in person. "When?"

"Two hours."

"Alright—" But the phone line was already dead.

CHAPTER 10

CASH POCKETED HIS PHONE AND listened to Nicola wander around the first floor of the beach house. They'd spent three gloriously boring weeks in the sweet paradise of South Carolina. Each day, a therapist came over and put him through the wringer of the recovery process.

Yeah, it was important. He got it. Really.

But—shit. His hand spun the phone—the one he wasn't allowed to stare at—in his pocket. The team was somewhere *undisclosed*, and that pissed him the hell off. He'd never cared where they were when he was on an off week having vacation, downtime, or whatever. But during an indefinite benching, Cash itched to get back into the field.

But every. Single. Damn. Day. The lady showed up to help him with crap that he *knew* he needed work on. Like vision and balance.

What the hell was a sniper without perfect damn vision and the ability to creep like a motherfuck, ghosting like a gust of wind? That there was even a question he might not be one hundred percent in the very near future stressed him out. Which caused a headache. Which made him angry. And the anger jumped his blood pressure, which made the therapist jot shit in her notebook and schedule a session for the next day.

Cash growled and tossed the phone on the bed before falling face-first beside it. If he lost his job, he'd lose his mind. Maybe his woman too? Nah, never. Nicola wouldn't walk away. He wondered what had made him think that.

Christ. His mind bounced too many places.

The thing was, though, she was perfection, and he was pretty fuckin' cocky when it came to being her better half. If he couldn't be the dude who jumped out of planes and could nail world-record-breaking sniper shots, who the hell was he?

A daddy... Cash fisted his hair. He had to be a provider, a daddy. Which meant he needed to get his act together.

Mind over matter. Concussions were bruises, the doc had said. *Sleep them off.* That was why he was stuck in a calm, soothing paradise with a beautiful woman and her slowly growing stomach: so that he could heal. Quietly. Without getting himself into trouble.

No guns.

No bombs.

No sniper shots.

No off-roading.

Nothing fun. He wasn't even supposed to go running yet. Seriously. He hadn't even touched his wife...no extracurricular activities allowed. Where was the rule book on that one? He touched her; he just didn't *touch* her...and at the moment, he could use a whole lot of touching her. Worshipping her body could melt any stress away.

Cash rolled over on the bed. "Hey, Nic. What are you doing?"

"I'm starving," she called from what sounded like the refrigerator. "Want to go get lunch?"

Feed the woman. He took a deep breath. Pregnancy had to be like a cold. Feed a cold, feed a pregnancy? No, that sounded all kinds of wrong. There had to be a book on this. *The Field Guide for First-Time Dads: Sniper Edition.*

"Yup. Food sounds good." Not as great as sex. But sate one need at a time. Man, did he feel like an asshole.

He pushed off the bed, and by the time he lumbered down the stairs, Nicola was standing by the door, beachy-looking bag draped over her shoulder, her blond hair loose and wavy, looking like a sun-kissed beach princess. That was the first moment he noticed her *glow*.

The girl had been a stunner their whole lives, but at the moment, she was just, like, whoa. He took two steps in one to get to her, slid both his arms under hers, and hauled her up for a kiss. "You're beautiful."

Nic laughed and giggled then kissed him back, and when she was out of his arms and on her feet, that glow in her cheeks was tinged with pink. Cash did not want to leave the house. Their bedroom was screaming for attention. But a different kind of alpha protectiveness kicked him in the gut, and it came down to basics— feed his woman and child—to the point where he wanted to beat his chest like a caveman. The overpowering need to take care of her in this new way almost knocked him over; Nicola was going to have a South Carolinian feast of food as soon as he could get her to town. "Let's go."

The pathway was sand covered until they hit the sidewalk. The beach house was far enough out of town that they didn't have neighbors but close enough that they could enjoy the walk. Nicola set the pace, and Cash scanned the horizon. Sand dunes, waves, and grassy knolls. He could hide in a million spots and take out a target. He glanced over his shoulder—just habit—to check the house in the fading distance. It was Jared's house. The security was maxed out. But just because security systems were in place didn't keep people from doing stupid things.

But this was paradise.

Still, his eyes jumped as though someone was watching him. He saw no one.

Nicola squeezed his hand. "Everything okay?" Worry colored her eyes.

Damn, everything was about healing, recovery, TBI, and making sure he wasn't cracking up, too tired, or losing his mind. "'Course, sweet girl."

Town came into sight, and still, he couldn't relax, but he could fake it. But he felt guilty. He'd never had to fake a thing to his wife. The Spidey tingles crawled down Cash's neck. Damn aftershocks. He couldn't even take his wife for a walk into town with that hypervigilant feeling that he should be on the alert. He stretched to alleviate the paranoia, bunched his shoulders, and tried to relax away the tension.

When his arms dropped and he fell back into stride with Nic again, her delicate fingers wound with his. "Don't lie. You okay?"

"Yeah." Busted. So maybe he couldn't get away with lying to her. Cash rubbed the back of his neck with his free hand, trying to shoo away the creepy crawlies. They were in coastal paradise. Nothing was wrong. If anything, he was bothered that the team was on a job that he knew shit about. "Just a tight muscle."

"Oh, that—*oh!*" She came to a standstill, staring

down, and panic flooded him. "Cash, here. Feel this. Now. Feel."

"What?" All he could feel were the stabby vibes that told him he should be armed.

"Cash. The baby."

Oh, right. Focus. Asshole. He closed his eyes and took a breath, trying to hone in and control everything as if this was a job, and the baby was a target.

"Cash?"

His eyes opened to a beautiful, worried Nic. "Sorry, I was trying to feel the baby."

"With your eyes closed?"

He shrugged a shoulder. That was how he'd concentrate before sighting a target. "Eyes open. Show me where."

Nicola moved her hands over his. "The baby's not moving this second." She pressed harder, and he could feel her insides. "Wait for it…"

"Whoa!" He reeled back as though his itchy trigger finger had detonated an early explosion.

"It's okay."

"I *touched* the baby."

"You did not, silly." Nicola pressed his palm to her stomach.

The baby pushed back, and Cash jumped again but this time without taking his hands away. "Holy shit, Nic."

"This time the baby touched you." Her eyes beamed.

Cash dropped to his knees in the middle of the sidewalk. "Can you hear me?"

Nic nodded. "Absolutely."

With both hands on the side of her stomach's swells, he glanced up at her. "That was insane. How often does that happen?"

"Just started."

He ran his hands over her stomach to the top of her small mound, leaned forward, and cupped his mouth. "I am your father."

"Cash." She tugged him up. "You're ridiculous."

"Parker would appreciate it."

"Alright, I want food. Time to feed us."

Damn if he didn't like how she used *us*. But as they hit the main street, the tingle of awareness came back. There were eyes on them. Pivoting, he saw no one out of place. Tourists. Townies. Everything was as it should be. Was he that off his game? *Paranoid much?* And if he was getting paranoid, what the hell kind of dad would that make him? He'd be like a dad who cried wolf—or who didn't see where the enemy lurked.

Shit, his temples pounded.

"Too much?" she asked. "We can head back. I can eat anything in the fridge. Literally, I can probably eat *everything* in the fridge."

Damn it to hell. His woman was questioning whether he was man enough to walk into town to grab grub. "Come on." He powered them into a restaurant where he knew he could find a table in the back corner and watch every single person walk in and out.

Paranoid? His eyes dropped to Nicola's stomach. Hell yeah, he was.

CHAPTER 11

LUNCH HAD NEARLY PUT NICOLA into a low-country seafood-and-grits coma, and the walk home seemed much longer than the one into town. Cash had gone from antsy to ecstatic to exhausted, all of which she'd been told to expect as they waded through the stages of traumatic-brain-injury recovery.

Off he went to nap—per her orders, which she blamed on doctor's orders—and she grabbed a book and went to the deck. The waves rolled on the beach, and the ocean-tinted breeze teased over Nicola, lightly blowing her maxi dress as she draped on the lounge chair. Off and on, she dozed while Cash was inside doing the same thing. But whether it was her stomach's increasing size or the baby kicking or pressing on her bladder, she couldn't get to sleep.

She pushed her sunglasses up her nose, knowing that she was lying even to herself. It wasn't that she couldn't sleep or get comfortable—both were true, but they were also lies. Something was off, and it wasn't her body or the baby. Readjusting on the lounge, she didn't want to be the crazy pregnant lady. But... Nicola scanned the vacant coastline beyond the deck. She didn't feel alone.

A few months ago, she would've grabbed her 9mm, woken her husband, and sought out the reason for her heebie-jeebies. But a baby in her tummy and a man whom she wanted to keep calm changed everything.

"That's it," she mumbled, letting the waves wash out her unconvincing lie. "My subconscious is testing me."

She made another quick scan of the perimeter. She squinted. *There's someone over there.* Nic didn't move or act as though she saw that person, who was probably a tourist out for a long walk along the beach—close to the reeds, standing still.

Nope. Red alarm. Something was wrong. *Shit. Okay.*

Never one to give up her cover, she stretched, and with faux-carefree laziness, watched another wave, eyeballing the figure in her peripheral vision, before slowly making her way inside.

As soon as the door clicked shut, she moved boots, running from one side of the house to the next. There was nothing like a Jared Westin beach house to keep things armed and dangerous. She hit the master bedroom, slamming to a slowdown, tiptoeing around a sleeping Cash, and grabbed the binoculars.

What else did she need? Hell, right now she was on a fact-finding mission. Back around the bed, and she was—

"Freeze."

Shit. Nicola turned around to face her very awake— husband. "Yeah?"

"What are you up to?"

"Had to get something." *And in a freakin' hurry.* "Go back to sleep."

"What?"

"Binoculars."

"Why?" He hadn't bothered to open his eyes or move.

"Jeez. Bird watching. Can I go now?"

Cash turned his head and opened his eyes. "Lie to me again, and see what happens."

Oh boy. "Go back to sleep."

"You ran through the house like you were up to something."

"I'll explain later." Telling him now would make his head explode, and that'd be bad for recovery and all. "My *bird watching* is time sensitive. Grill me later. Please?"

His eyes narrowed. "You have the Spidey senses too." He pushed out of bed, feeling along the side of the nightstand until he retrieved a Glock 9.

"Cash Garrison!"

He stood up, pausing for what had to be a second longer than his old norm. "Let's go."

"The doctor said no loud noise, no percussive forces. He *stipulated* no gunfire."

"Walk and talk, sweet girl."

"Shit, you obnoxious alpha man."

"You dangerous pregnant woman," he grumbled. "Scoot your booty, baby."

She obeyed because he was already moving. "There's a man a thousand yards away, posted in the sand dunes." They moved smoothly, as though she weren't pregnant and he hadn't been in a TBI clinic. They were two of a kind. Without speaking, they intuitively flowed, taking the same path, taking their positions in the house, and looking out windows without being seen.

She scanned the perimeter. The man in the dunes was gone. Cash did a walk-around with his weapon handy but out of sight. He flicked the lock on the door, giving Nicola an eye for not doing so when she'd opted to smoothly slip in then run like hell for the binoculars, and finished checking the inside of the house.

Nicola heard the garage door open and close as he left her alone for twenty minutes, and then Cash reappeared, walking up the back-deck stairs. He knocked on the door, and she let him in. Both stayed silent; she put her binoculars on the kitchen table, and he placed the Glock there, within reach.

"So…" she said, sitting down. There were a hundred ways this conversation could go. She was crazy. They were nuts together. Field withdrawal had made them insane, or her hormones and his concussion had joined forces to send them to the looney bin.

"What'd he look like?"

"I didn't get a good look."

Cash pinched the bridge of his nose. "At least you got a look."

"Meaning?"

He shrugged and ran a fist into his rumpled hair.

Nicola rested her hand on her stomach. "People are going to think we've lost our marbles."

Cash's eyes narrowed. He shook his head. "Nah, something's up."

The determination in his face matched the fear in her tummy. He would maim, kill, and destroy whatever threatened his wife and child—even if it hurt him, which it would likely do. A simple gunshot reverb could set back his rehab. The idea of Cash in an altercation scared the hell out of her.

"Do you want to go home?" she asked.

His jaw flexed. "Do I want to run home because my wife saw a man in the sand who scared her?" He tilted his head. "How hard do you think I was hit in the head, Nic?"

"That's not what I meant."

"Want me to call Jared, see if someone can come down and protect you? Maybe Roman can come sit up nights and watch out for his little sis."

"Don't be an asshole, Cash."

He shook his head, glaring. "Seriously. Not like I don't have shit to deal with. 'Don't shoot guns. Don't get in fights.' That's what I do for a living!"

Her eyes went wide. Okay. Mood swings. Anger. It was like a TBI checklist playing out live in front of her. "I didn't mean to upset you."

"God. Damn. This is making my head pound."

"Maybe lie down. I didn't mean to wake you."

The chair scraped across the floor when he pushed back. "Right. Sure. Let my pregnant wife run around playing caped crusader to the man in the bushes. I'm the fucking father-to-be of the year."

"Cash, that's not…"

He stormed out of the room, leaving the 9mm and binoculars on the table and her in tears.

CHAPTER 12

"PARKER," CASH GROWLED INTO THE phone. "I don't give two shits who you have to murder or maim to get me on the line with Boss Man, but *make it happen.*"

"He's—"

"Right now, goddamn it."

"Jesus fucking Christ, Cash. Calm the fuck down."

"I am calm. You want to see me not calm? There will be a bloodbath in Podunk, South Carolina, and his perfect little beach house will be a crime scene. Get Jared on the damn phone."

"Is everything okay with you and Nic?" Parker asked as though proposing to crawl through the phone line and wage war to protect Titan's pregnant spy.

"Insinuate again that there's a problem with me and my wife's safety—"

"That was a dick move," Parker apologized. "Just explain."

CRISTIN HARBER

"For fuck's sake. It's an unsecure line, asshole. You know that better than me. I have a problem. If I can't talk to him, figure out how I'm supposed to talk to you. Shit."

Parker sighed. "You know what benched means? I have strict orders to not engage with you. At all."

"Someone's sniffing around here. I've got the vibe, and before you say one damn word about post-traumatic bullshit, I am not wrong."

"Cash—"

"Nic saw a guy—"

"*Cash*—"

"I've got the vibe."

"Dude, listen—"

"It's my motherfucking woman and child. So no, you listen. Get Jared on the phone now, or patch me through to a goddamn secure line, and *you* listen then relay what you need to. Do you understand?"

Parker paused a beat. "Yeah. My bad. Hang tight."

Cash dropped his forehead to his shaking palm, noticing the twinge of perspiration, and then scrubbed his face. A garbled noise ate into the phone line.

Parker's voice broke the static. "Secure line."

"Heard vacation bliss has a hiccup." Boss Man's voice cut in and out, echoing. "What do you need?"

The tension in his neck was instantly dispelled, and without thinking, Cash began to rattle off a shopping list that would make the NSA jealous.

86

"Done."

With the Jared stamp of approval, Cash knew by the next morning he'd have satellite feeds and thermal imaging of every sand dune a thousand yards in any direction. If a seagull took a piss, if a fish jumped out of the water, Cash would know about it. That promise of intel soothed his soul, and he went to double-check the Titan-esque security system installed on the beach house and then go find his wife. *Like hell she's sleeping alone.*

CHAPTER 13

NICOLA WOKE, CLINGING TO A blanket tucked under her chin. She'd cried herself to sleep on the couch, and hours must have passed because the sun was gone and the room was a deep shade of hours-gone-by. Only a few lights from a hallway were on, and she couldn't remember grabbing the blanket, but it did something nice to ward off the loneliness of dozing on the couch.

Today sucked. Fighting with Cash, her paranoia—or maybe reality—whatever it was had been just too much to handle. She shifted on the couch, and a whiff of man caught her attention, as did the light breath of a snore—Cash, asleep on the floor at the base of the couch.

Of course, she shouldn't have doubted him. Fight or not, he couldn't have been more of a perfect man. A hardheaded, alpha protector of a man, but one who bugged the snot out of her, made her smile, and who'd sleep on the floor next to the couch when she didn't come to bed.

God, he was a good one, and to think she'd almost lost him...

He had a pillow and a blanket and must've been responsible for her blanket too. "I hate fighting with you." No answer, so maybe his Spidey senses were turned off for the moment. Nicola reached down and found his hand. "Come here."

Awakening, he focused his blue eyes on her in the shadowy dark. "Hey."

"Don't sleep on the floor."

He chuckled, low and sexy. "Don't sleep on the couch, and I won't have that problem."

"Come up here. You'll still fit." She pulled him up, and with just a tug, her heart was happy, and he was under the blanket.

He kissed the back of her head. "Someone wants to find one of us, sweet girl."

"Doesn't make sense."

"Of course it does. We have a laundry list of enemies. It's only a matter of time." He kissed the back of her neck softly, letting his lips linger. "No one will hurt you."

"I know."

His tongue lingered where his lips had been, and she sighed, half melting into him, half awakening. Weeks of feeling ill and then days that felt like centuries had made her numb without realizing, but buried in the blankets, feeling safe and secure, loved and cared for, she felt a flood of sexuality in her blood. It came with an unexpected intensity and warmness.

"That feels nice." Her back arched.

"Good." Cash brushed her hair away from her neck and tugged her shirt over her shoulder, drifting languid, sleepy kisses at a maddeningly slow pace from ear to shoulder and back again. "Take the dress off, Nic."

Pushing up out of their blanket cocoon, his hands found her stomach and lifted the long sundress before she had a chance to do it. Nicola unhooked her bra, and Cash enveloped her, pressing her back to his chest, spooning them together under the cashmere blanket. The palm of his hand swept across her flesh, back and forth, and every little touch ignited sparks a thousand times more sensitive than she'd ever before had. Nicola squirmed, in heaven.

"What, are you ticklish now?" he whispered against her earlobe.

And, good God, pregnancy hormones might be the greatest thing for sex since…since God made Cash Garrison. "Just…" Her voice shook. "We haven't since I was pregnant."

His hand paused. They'd passed the time frame in which he had to be careful about TBI-related *sex injuries*, whatever that meant, but he hadn't thought about *pregnant* sex. "We shouldn't?"

"If you dare stop, I will strangle you."

His laugh ran down her spine. "Ten-four, sweet girl."

"I think it's called heightened awareness."

"So if I do this…" He palmed her breast, letting his thumb gently rub her erect nipple.

"Yeah, if you do that…" She squirmed against him, aware of her breathy nonresponse and not caring.

His strong fingers massaged her mound, and Nicola gasped.

"Christ, Nic." His voice had dropped too. With lips close to her ear, Cash sounded equal parts aroused and curious, as though heaven had sent him his favorite playground. He flicked her earlobe with his tongue then grabbed it with his teeth, sucking it into his mouth, kissing the spot that he'd memorized years ago as one of her hot buttons.

With his fingers plucking her nipple, his tongue behind her ear, and his erection pressed against her ass, Nicola could stay buried in blanketed bliss, bordering on an almost orgasm without him even touching between her legs.

Heat blossomed inside her body at the thought. *Wow.* Hormones could be a curse, but at that moment, they were a blessing. She was wet beyond a doubt, moaning for her man, and enjoying every sensation— from the light scratch of his chest hair pressed against her back to the heavy sound of his breath.

Cash shifted, his hand dropping to the swell of her belly. "Beautiful. You with more curves." He kissed her bicep and moved to her breast, sucking the tip into his warm mouth. "Tits that I want to bury myself in."

She wriggled, pushing herself under him, letting his massive hulk cover her body, holding against her but not smothering her. He'd long ago mastered that perfect balance of dominance and carefulness that was almost a requirement for someone so strong, long, and muscled, but it always came coupled with sexy gentleness.

But now that she was pregnant, he'd upped his game. Cash Garrison was *worshipping* her body as only an alpha male could do. There was a mix of pure, unadulterated possession, longing, love, and need all rolled up in one sexually driven man intent on making her batshit crazy. It was working.

His hands skimmed over her taut stomach. Every day, she had to put lotion on it. The skin itched from where it was growing and stretching and from where the baby was kicking. She hadn't been sure if it was pretty or sexy, but in the shaded light with him dropping to his knees in front of her, her pregnant stomach next to his golden hair and scruffy cheeks, those blue-blue eyes that she could picture in any shade of the dark—that was gorgeous.

Goosebumps popped on her stomach where his hands were. He chased them down with kisses, letting his palms rest on her hips. "I need you naked, baby."

Nicola lifted her hips, and he tugged down her panties.

He snaked a hand behind her head, pulling her down for a kiss that could draw a climax out. He didn't stop. His tongue delved into her mouth, and he ate at her lips, breathing in every breath she tried for. Nicola pressed to him, widening her legs to get closer, to wrap her arms around him, to taste him, to love him, to consume him in every possible way she could think of—his free hand stroked her pussy, and she bucked and balked. Arched and moaned. Cash gripped the back of her head, forcing her still, greedily owning that kiss, and she groaned and nodded, needing him to touch her harder and kiss her longer.

"Don't stop." She bit through the kiss.

He didn't bother with words. Her legs were wide, and his fingers were fast, sliding the seams of her needy lips. Nicola flexed her hips, trying for more, begging for his fingers to push inside.

Fuck it. He wouldn't let her dictate a thing. Nicola gasped, giving up the moment, threading her hands into his hair and holding his mouth to hers. As though that had been the key, he thrust two fingers into her body.

She couldn't help it. Her hands fell loose, and her body went lax. The world spun on that simple invasion, and Cash laid her back on the couch. "Such a sweet girl."

She nodded because she was putty—agreement was

all there was. His mouth dropped to her chest, sucking one tit then the next as he fingered her pussy and teased her clit. There was nothing slow about it. What started out strong went to insane.

"God. Cash." She thrashed on the couch, dragging one leg up as he kneeled on the floor. "Please."

Clawing on the couch cushions, she thought there might not have been an orgasm this strong ever in her life. He curled his fingers inside her body and moved his mouth lower, kissing over her stomach until his lips found her clit. "Cash, please."

He threw her other leg over his shoulder and buried his face between her legs. His scratchy cheeks abraded her sensitive lips. Her clitoris screamed in pleasure as he sucked deep and swirled his tongue, and his fingers fucked her as she tightened, tightened, tightened and—

"Cash." She came, calling his name.

He thrust his fingers in time with each rippling wave of orgasm, his tongue lapping and licking, her body shaking at the response. Tears seeped out her eyes. Sniffles too. Stars were in her head, the explosion of the climax rocketing from toes to fingertips, and she shook…because she was crying and had no idea why.

Goddamn hormones. But wasn't it just the best orgasm ever. With the best man ever.

"I love you." She sniffled and whispered and found herself speaking against his lips as he kissed her sweetly.

CRISTIN HARBER

Who knew where those lost seconds went, but now he was over her body. "Always, baby. What's with the tears?"

She laughed. "I have no freaking clue."

His forehead touched hers, and their eyes locked. "You sure?"

"Best orgasm of my life, maybe?"

"I don't know about that." His lazy half grin almost looked as though it had been issued a challenge. "Top five?"

"Shut up," she teased, but he caught her with another kiss.

"Don't fight with me again or fall asleep elsewhere."

Nodding, she agreed, hooking her fingers in the drawstrings of his pajama pants, tugging them lower. "Deal. We're not done making up, are we?"

"Not a chance. I made you cry. Don't know how I feel about that." He kissed her cheek, nuzzling into her hair.

"I didn't cry. Just tears. *Very* good tears."

Cash scooped her into his arms, grabbed the blanket, and threw it over the back of the couch. "You're up, I'm down."

Before she could think, he had her straddling him with the blanket wrapped around her. Then he lifted her a bit so he could tug down his pajama pants. There was nothing sexier than her husband, golden tan with hair mussed from sending her to orgasm, lying in front of her, his cock gorgeously thick and him staring, waiting with those beautiful, boyish looks, too cocky for words, too sweet for his own good. She stacked her hands on his hardened length and watched his eyes stutter closed as she gripped him and stroked, thumbing the top of his head in that special place that made him turn to mush, right under the crown.

That she could do that to him, the guy who was God's gift to women—who, even when her belly poked out, still drank her up—made him more than someone to marry. He was the one to spend forever with.

His eyes were sealed and his head pressed back into the pillow. Nicola rose on her knees and guided his shaft between her legs. Cash sucked air as his blunt head made contact with her needy, wet flesh, and she hungrily inched herself onto his cock, letting the invasion stretch her, feeling the slight difference of pregnancy sex and the pressure from within her body.

"Nicola?"

She hadn't realized her eyes were closed and her lips had parted. "Yeah?"

"You okay, baby?"

Nodding, she tested how true that was. Whoa. Yes. Very okay. Her breaths shook. "Yeah. This is good."

His hands went to her sides, where he so often had held her as she fucked him, and his strong fingers were expertly gentle. He wasn't too careful but wouldn't come close to bruising her. But, *God,* he commanded her hips to sway, and they did. Her lungs couldn't fill deep enough to keep away that moaning, gasping, needing breath that fell from her lips. "Cash, this is...so..."

His fingers gripped tighter on her hips as she relaxed and, now completely accustomed to his length, slipped back and forth on his shaft, riding him as her heavier-than-normal breasts tingled with newfound arousal. He dropped a hand to her butt cheek, squeezing it while the fingers of his free hand teased her clit.

"Sweet Jesus." Cash's low growl of a curse came as his hips began to flex just a little. Just enough. Meeting her stride, letting her still dictate, he sent her straight to the pearly gates of almost orgasmic overload.

Nicola ground down on him, and his mouth gaped.

"Killing me, Nic."

"Yes," she panted.

He reached for her face, threading his hands into her hair, pulling her into a kiss, and took over, thrusting into her body, and she cried as the orgasm hit hard. Shaking and bucking, Cash kissed her harder, holding her to his chest, owning her kiss, and he came too, hot and deep inside. Each thrust felt better than the last as he slowed.

They were tangled—arms and legs, locked lips and heavy breaths—pulsing, sated, and still attached at the hips. She went limp as bliss rolled from deep inside her belly to the far reaches of her fingertips and toes.

Cash twisted their bodies and lay over her without crushing, his mouth unmoving and not kissing but not leaving hers, and their hearts slammed back and forth, talking in unspoken words.

"I…" He inched back, brushing the hair off her cheeks, then kissed her forehead, letting his love-swollen lips linger. "Need you as much as I love you."

Thank God for her husband. "You just made my soul smile."

CHAPTER 14

THREE DAYS HAD TICKED BY, and Nicola and he had left the lack of bad vibes unsaid. Whoever had been watching them was gone. Today something was different in the air. There was a reason both had been called to their careers. They possessed a sixth sense where doom and gloom were concerned.

"You check the imaging?" Nicola casually sipped her tea—which the local coffee shop had assured her a dozen times was decaf—but her cool and laid-back act wasn't fooling him.

"Yup."

"The baby's Spidey senses are tingling."

His eyes dropped to her stomach. "Guess it runs in the genes, huh?"

"HQ have any idea?"

"On who's snooping around?" He shook his head. "But if all three of our Spidey senses are humming, we'll know soon enough. The White House has less security protocol per square inch than we're running in this place, so—"

Both their phones lit with an alert.

Her eyebrows went up, and she met his I-knew-it gaze. Cash swiped the screen of his phone, knowing that they'd see more than a roaming seagull or a wind-tossed piece of trash. Sure enough, in the distance, thermal imaging picked up two men burrowing into a sandy position on the bank of a dune. "Get comfy, assholes. Make it a nice place to die."

"Do you want to call the cops?" She sipped her tea.

Cash scoffed. "Do you?"

She put her lips to the mug. "Nope. Just checking on that injured brain of yours."

He leaned over to kiss her. "Glad my interest in avoiding law enforcement means I'm doing better."

"Avoid reinjury. Okay?"

"I don't have to convince you to stay put?"

"Not a chance in the world unless you need backup, in which case, I'm calling Jared rather than the cops."

"Good girl." He kissed her again. "Time to go find out who these fuckers are and what they want."

Nicola smacked his butt as he walked by, and it was equally unnerving and calming that they were back to who they were. She might be pregnant, and he might be on the upside of TBI, but they were still trained operatives, lethal and dangerous and more able to protect house and hearth than most standard operators.

Cash cracked his knuckles and suited up with what he'd already scoured the house for: two handguns, extra ammo, a throwing knife, serrated blade, and a fist full of flexi-cuffs. They could never be too careful or overprepared.

He slunk out of the house and relocked it then re-engaged the security system. With the binoculars spotting the men, Cash backed around, letting the wind mask the sound of his footsteps, and he melted into the brush and weeds. Sniper training often served him well, and this was no exception. His target never saw him coming.

Cash centered, visualized his targets, saw them as dead. One was a light-haired man who had a military haircut with a week or two of overgrowth. The other was a dark-haired man in a poor prone field position. His build was athletic, but he clearly had no tactical training. They both might be killers, and neither one was what Cash would call comfortable in the sand dune—they made rookie mistakes all over the place—but Light Hair looked more experienced than Dark Hair.

Assessment done, he lunged.

Landed.

Attacked.

With a choke hold on the dark-haired man, who was definitely athletic, Cash had the upper hand. His mark had been trained at one time, but in the sand and the brush, the man couldn't get his footing. The other man stuttered in his decision to help before going for Cash's back. A single punch over his shoulder knocked the light-haired man to the dune.

Dark Hair and Cash rolled down a hill; the other man, capable but untrained, couldn't handle the elements, inhaling the sand and letting it scrape into his eyes. Cash gained the momentum, ducking a blind punch. He straddled the attacker and drilled two fists, one and two. Lights out.

God. Damn. Cash blinked.

The morning sun shone overhead, and there was no question of what Cash looked down on. He reached into his back pocket, grabbing the flexi-ties and keeping an eye on the other unconscious man on top of the hill, then patted down the asshole in front of him, removing weapons before he pulled out his cell phone.

Cash wanted to puke. Parker answered on the first ring. "What the fuck is going on? We're watching—"

Cash ran his hand over his face, forgetting that Titan had likely seen everything, and if he took any punches, they were going to know about it. That didn't matter at the moment. He yanked the guy by his shirt, shaking him for the satellite field. "This guy?" He shook him harder, angrier than he'd been in years. In *decades*. "He's a fucking Gianori mobster."

He knew them all. Knew their faces. Knew their

children, their houses, their names, their wives and cousins and lawyers and moles and snitches. He'd been studying them for a decade. Cash knew everything about the Gianori mob because they would forever want to kill his wife.

CHAPTER 15

NESTING SHOULDN'T OCCUR IN THE second trimester of pregnancy in someone else's house—right? But nerves were driving Nicola to the point of polishing Jared and Sugar's beach bungalow. Nic had dusted though the place was speck free and apparently had a force of security-clearance-level housekeepers who would pop in while she and Cash were out and tidy the hell out of the house.

Only Jared Westin would have a security-clearance brigade of maids.

But for the moment, puttering around the house with a perfectly clean rag alleviated Nicola's nerves. It wasn't that Cash went off to take care of business. Her concern was that he had been gone a very long time *after* fists had been thrown.

Nicola had watched the entire show on her phone. Thermal imaging hadn't shown her the greatest picture, but she liked his approach. She smiled when he dodged swings, cringed when the other guy rolled on top of him, and triumphed when he took down the two men.

But then he sat there. Why wasn't he hauling their bound intruders in? He wouldn't answer her calls. He was obviously on the phone with Titan, so what was the deal?

Easy answer: those two men had wanted *her*, and her husband was keeping them at bay.

Or she was deluded by hormones, and the world didn't revolve around her; Cash was simply waiting for cops in the land of beach and sun. They likely didn't have a lot of violent crime in the area, and bike patrol couldn't pick up two…two what? Stalkers?

Or maybe they were mobsters. That was her subconscious go-to fear and had been for almost a third of her life.

She scrubbed the hell out of a nonexistent spot on the kitchen counter. Her calls to Titan were left unanswered as well. Everyone was keeping her out of the loop, and that did nothing to ease her concerns.

Best-case scenario was that they were a couple of goofs from town who had hit on her a few weeks ago when she was wearing a billowing dress that hid her starting-to-show belly and carrying a bag of groceries that covered her wedding band. But Cash wouldn't stay out there for hours with a couple of townie bozos. He also would not knock them out and tie them up.

Worst-case scenario… Nicola folded and refolded the cloth. Her subconscious was in overdrive, screaming, "Oh, crap!" The Gianori family would be the worst-case scenario. They'd dictated her life for years, and why weren't they her first thought, her *every* thought? *Shit.*

She picked up the phone and called Cash. No answer.

She dialed Titan. No answer.

Fuck it. She texted her husband.

It's them, isn't it? Gianori?

Nicola put the phone down and stared, willing it to ring, and the screen lit up less than a minute later. If it were the mob, why wouldn't they just kill her? Why spend days scouting her? So maybe it was just random kids who were a little too nosy. Nothing made sense.

"Hey." His strained voice was all the answer she needed.

"Shit." That tone of voice said there was nothing local or accidental about the men Cash had in his custody. He had called only when she had figured it out. Gianori.

"We're handling it, sweet girl. Take it easy."

"I don't want you to handle it for me. I want you to tell me what's going on so that *we* handle it together. *I've* handled them for years on my own!"

"Nicola, baby." Cash's voice was low and calm but not enough to soothe her. "Parker has eyes on the house. If anything was to change, if a crab was to scuttle its ass too close to the house, he'd be on the phone with you in a hot second, and you'd know about it. But for now, give me a minute."

"You're sitting in the sand dunes with two mobsters waiting on what?"

"A pickup from a friendly."

Her head dropped into her hand. "How long will you be gone?"

"I'm not going anywhere. Just them, and then I'm headed back to you."

Oh... "Then what do we do? Where there's one Gianori, there's more."

"My vote is to napalm their houses and car-bomb any survivors. Taste of their own medicine." He paused. "I, however, was outvoted."

She saw merit in Cash's point of view but also voted for keeping him out of jail. "So?"

"The simple answer is I don't know. Jared has someone special coming in for these two, then we talk. Yeah?"

She nodded even though he couldn't see her.

"Nicola?"

"Yes."

"I promise you: this is the last of it. Believe me?"

"Always." She pressed the screen and tossed the

phone on the counter then refolded the cloth but tossed it too. Her chest was tight, and her eyes closed as she dragged in a deep breath, praying that it would loosen the rigid hold that fear had on her throat.

The breathing didn't work. Nicola smoothed her palms over her stomach. "Daddy said it'll be okay. Everything will be fine."

This was the first pang of mommy guilt. She was bringing a child into the world when there was a mob that for more than a decade had wanted to see her dead. If that wasn't a selfish act, what was? Nicola shuffled to the master bedroom, tears streaming down her face as she rubbed her belly, promising their baby that everything would be fine, that Daddy would fix all and would be home soon, safe and sound.

Curling under the blankets, hands still on her belly, mommy guilt firmly in place, she began to drift to sleep while promising her child the world.

CHAPTER 16

THERE WAS NOTHING MORE BEAUTIFUL than watching Nicola sleep. He'd thought that when he first got her back into his bed. But this was different. Before, the sight of her had been sexy as all fuck. Now, propped on her side, the blanket draped over her bulging stomach, that was…his world.

His phone buzzed, and Jared's name appeared on screen. Cash answered as he headed into the hall. "Hey."

"You're on speaker. Parker, Roman, and Rocco."

Hellos were grumbled.

Jared continued, "The brain trust has an idea and, well, yeah, shit. I think this might work."

I think this might work. Not exactly a strong endorsement. "Don't blow me over with confidence, Boss Man."

"Bianca Gianori—"

"*Bianca*? A girl?" Cash tried to picture a woman behind anything he knew in the Gianori world and couldn't. Then he decided not taking the women into account would be his Achilles' heel. Women were just as evil as men.

"Don't be a sexist. Mobsters can be chicks," Jared shot back.

"Fine." Cash didn't care.

"Back to the point." Jared cleared his throat. "She's actually not mobbed up but, rather, drugged out. Fell face-first into a pile of Colombia's best. Both coke and cock."

Cash raised his eyebrows. "So?"

"We make a deal. Bianca for Nicola. Titan finds this Bianca chick, assuming she's still alive and attached to the pants of some cartel kingpin, and brings her home."

"Exchange Bianca for Nicola?" Cash repeated.

"Yeah. They want their blood back. We get an agreement to walk away from Nicola. Forever."

"Bianca will be on the first flight back to Colombia."

"Or street corner for cocaine," Roman added.

Jared grumbled. "We throw in for detox. Rehab. I don't know."

"They sleep on bags of money. They don't need that," Rocco said. "But...it likely goes against their grain."

114

"Exactly," Roman agreed. "They won't detox her. Too risky."

"What was your suggestion?" Jared asked Roman.

"I liked Cash's car-bomb plan."

"Christ." Jared paused. "Let's keep it legal. As legal as we can with these fuckers. No body counts, as best we can help it. Other ideas?"

"What are you going to do?" Cash asked. "Just go down and grab her? Fly her back to the States?"

"Basically," Parker answered. "With some medical provisions so she doesn't detox and die in flight. But yes."

"Why did she leave in the first place? Hates her folks? Smart enough to hate all things Gianori?"

"Nope. She was a kept Gianori princess, from what we can tell. But now she has a cartel boyfriend that won't let her come home and a liking for very, *very* good cocaine that comes right from the source."

"Huh." Cash rubbed his face. This wasn't going to work, but he could—

"Hey," Nicola said, leaning against the living-room wall.

"Guys, hang on a second." He put the phone on mute. "I didn't mean to wake you."

"You didn't; it was just time. So…" She looked pointedly at the phone.

"How much did you hear?"

"Enough to know that won't work to clear my debt with the Gianori mob."

His head dropped. "Yeah, I know."

"It won't work unless she wants to stay home, wants to get clean."

"That's a lot to bank your future on, Nicola."

She nodded. "Put them on speaker."

Cash swiped the screen. "Nic's here."

"Hey, Princess. Causing trouble, as always?" Jared laughed-slash-grumbled.

"You know it."

"Alright," Cash interrupted. "Nic has a good point, and that is unless this girl wants to get clean, staying home will never work. Gianori assholes won't hold up their end of the deal."

"Agree," Parker's voice carried through the line. "From what I've been able to dig up, she's *tried* unsuccessfully to *vacation* on her own a few times in the last year. Each time, she never made it to the airport."

"You're thinking our coked-up mob girl is trying to go home?" Nicola asked.

"Yes," Parker said. "But cartel boyfriend decides no."

"Hmmm." Nicola gave Cash a look. "If it was as easy as grabbing her and taking her home, why haven't they done that?"

A collective grumble erupted from the other side of the phone line.

"Point of concern and contention," Jared finally

announced. "Probably our largest stumbling block to having the Gianoris agree to this. There's likely a business partnership we do not know about that stands in the way of bringing one of their own home."

Cash's gut curled. Assholes. They would give up their children to make a dollar. So typical of what he knew of them, yet it still hurt. Why would Bianca even want to go home to that? Well, hell, because home was home, and sometimes a person couldn't help who they loved.

Nicola was still eyeballing the shit out of him. He put the phone on mute. "What?"

"Go down there."

The words were so unexpected he recoiled. "What?"

"Go."

"To kidnap a drug-addicted chick?" Yeah, that sounded like hell. To grab a detoxing, struggling woman and drag her onto a plane.

"No. All you do is make the offer. Cash, you can sweet-talk anyone into anything."

Not sure that's a compliment or not... "I'm benched."

"Yeah, you just knocked two guys out." She shook her head. "Never mind. That's an awful idea."

His cocky smile and a puffed-out chest came out of nowhere. Damn, he loved it when his wife complimented him.

"Ignore me," she mumbled. "And unmute. Saying it out loud sounded different than it did in my head."

"It's my head that's the issue." He tapped his temple. "I'm in this for the long haul. Sweet-talk might not go well, and…" If a coked-out lunatic hit him in the head, he didn't want to lose all of his marbles because of some Gianori piece of shit. They'd already fucked up so many pieces of his life.

"Unmute the phone."

"But you're onto something." He had no idea if he wanted to debate this with everyone listening, but he needed to treat her as a teammate, not as his wife. The distinction killed him at times.

"I'm not," she insisted. "I'm sorry I even planted the idea."

Cash rubbed his brow. "This is the thing: if there's one group of people I trust to keep me safe"—he motioned to the phone—"it's them. I'm as good with words as with my weapon, and I *need* a job. I'm going nuts."

Nicola's jaw flexed as she shook her head. "Really. It was wrong of me to say anything. I don't know what I was thinking. I *wasn't* thinking. Okay?"

"I get on the plane and sweet-talk. That's it. The guys do the heavy lifting."

"She's a cokehead, a cartel piece of arm candy, likely surrounded by bodyguards and volatile." Nicola moved close and kissed the top of his head. "If something goes wrong, I will die alongside you. You get that, right?"

Cash took her hands in his. "They don't have a better idea. If they did, you and I wouldn't be tossing this BS back and forth." He pressed his palm to her stomach. "I'll be fine, and I'll do what it takes to come home, no problem. But I can't let this linger over us. Do you get that?"

Her eyes squeezed shut. "Cash…" She dropped her head back as he let both his hands rest on her stomach. "I shouldn't have said anything."

"If you didn't, we wouldn't have a plan."

"We *don't*."

"Sweet girl, *we do*."

Nicola brought her gaze back to him, blond hair falling forward. "Unmute the phone." He did as she licked her lips and closed her eyes again. "Bring Cash to Bianca. He can talk an Eskimo into the AC business."

The line was eerily quiet.

Nicola dropped her hands on top of his. "A few minutes with him, she'll hop on the plane willingly, go to her family, enroll in detox and rehab, and then she will *stay* in the US."

There was a grumbling of tentative approval.

Nic went in for the kill. "We have a good chance they'll release their grudge against me. Getting Bianca home and clean would be a good deal for them. They'd take it."

Her breaths were short, and he tugged her into his lap as unsteady nerves seemed to take hold of her. Cash could sense that everyone was working over the interesting offer of him as an asset. She was his number-one protector. If Nicola would put him on a job, then Jared had to consider it.

"Cash? You up to it?" Jared asked. "You smile and wink, do your magic, and if all goes well, Bianca Gianori gets on a plane, and you have a full military escort protecting you in case someone tries to stop that from happening. And if she balks, we grab her anyway, then you have a plane ride to talk sense into her. Plan A and B, rolled into one."

They exchanged glances, and Nic gave him the thumbs-up.

"Yeah, we're a go from here," Cash said.

A few seconds of mumbling from the other side, and Jared responded the same. "Delta team's coming in to escort Nicola to Titan HQ. Sugar will be here along with Beth and Parker. Cash, pack a go-bag, and Parker, tell him where we'll pick him up. See you in South America."

The screen blinked, showing that the call had ended.

Nicola laughed nervously. "Full Delta escort for me, huh?"

"How about that?" he grumbled, not wanting to leave her side. "But it will finally be over."

"And that will be some kind of sweet relief."

CHAPTER 17

BIANCA GIANORI COULDN'T HAVE LOOKED more out of place if she tried, Cash decided as he watched her sit in a bar in Colombia with her pale skin, deep Italian black hair, and dark circles that were painted underneath her sunken eyes. Exhaustion and malnourishment were evident even as expensive clothes hung on her shaky frame.

A coked-out cartel floozy. There were several of them in the room, making it apparent that whoever their cartel boyfriend was, he wasn't smitten with a single one of them. He was a collector of people. *Sad...*

Cash pulled up a bar stool next to the girl. She was twenty-three years old, but life had run her over, and a quick glance might've pegged her as being in her late thirties. "Heya, sunshine."

Her head tilted, and an eager, lonely smile shone. "You're an American."

"How 'bout that?" He tugged his cowboy hat in a way that did something to women, and smiled halfway. "You are too?"

She nodded and toyed with a beer bottle, the label long since picked off. "Welcome to this crazy country."

He made her laugh and smile, and it killed him because it was too easy. No one had spent a moment's time to make this poor kid smile in so long. She was hungry for conversation and attention. Not even the sexual kind. "You need a friend."

She paused, and her eyes dropped to her beer bottle. *That* was apparently her friend. Not that going home to Gianori was good, but it was better than this, and no one said she had to be a criminal if she went home to her family.

"I have to tell you something—what's your name?"

She shrugged. "Bianca."

"And you're going to get upset, but I want you to remember how great it feels to have had a friend for the last few minutes."

Warily, she inched back. "What?"

"My name is Cash."

"Okay."

"I know your family, and I'm here to help."

She recoiled, almost sliding off the bar stool, but he wrapped one arm around her back while the other steadied her forearm on the bar.

"Take a deep breath. This is not a test. You are

not in trouble. I am a safe place. A good person."

Bianca blinked, her eyelashes going rapid fire.

"I'm going to take my hands off you now. *Don't run*, sunshine. I have something to ask you."

"Okay," she whispered, voice shaking. She looked terrified.

"Is it fear of losing the drugs, or were you hurt when you tried to go home?"

The rapid blinking stopped, and her eyeballs nearly popped out of her head. "How, um, I…"

Cash reached into his pocket, pulling out a business card for Titan Group. "If you don't take me up on what I'm about to offer, call this number, day or night, and you will have help."

"Who are you?"

"I'm the American named Cash." He flashed his smile and winked. "Walk out with me. We're getting on a plane. Your parents are waiting for you, and there's a way to get through the shakes, sweats, and pukes without having to deal with detox."

"Bullshit," she whispered.

"There are also…" He stretched, gently nodding his head. "Two of my men in here and several outside. No one can stop you if you decide it's time to go home, that you're done with this shitty cantina and snorting away your life."

She cringed.

"I know it feels good at that moment, sunshine.

That you crave it. Taste it. Want it. Need it."

Her eyes watered.

"Can't live without it."

She nodded.

He put his hand on the bar. "But you can sure as fuck try."

Bianca stared at his hand as though it were green and gross.

"Grab on, sunshine. I'm your ticket to tomorrow."

She didn't move.

"Take a breath and do it."

One little, teeny-tiny breath came before a cold, bony hand landed in his much larger one. "That's my girl." Cash curled his fingers around hers. "Time to get you home."

CHAPTER 18

SHAKING KNEES WEREN'T NICOLA'S THING. Picking imaginary lint off her shirt, fidgeting, or nodding on the phone when no one could see her—those were her things. But she had an iron rod for a backbone and impenetrable courage. Having wobbly spaghetti legs was a new thing. So was standing in front of Emilio Gianori Junior, the man who had ordered a hit on her—*knowing* she was with child.

The fucker. Her knees stopped shaking. Those nerves could be expected, but they were gone. The reminder that he wanted to murder her baby made them a distant memory. "You wanted to see me, so now you've seen me."

"You've become quite the little force to be reckoned with, haven't you, Mrs. Garrison?"

Nicola took a step forward. Jared and Cash, who had flanked her, remained in place. "When I was in college, that was a shitty situation of wrong place, wrong time. That *sucked*, if there ever was such a reason to use such a basic, all-encompassing word." She took another step forward. "But I didn't ask for what happened to me. I didn't go after you—I didn't want that. I did what I did to stay alive. I left my family, my loved ones, my life to stay away from you." She spun on her heel, exaggerating her out-thrown arms. "Now look. It's still on me, all because one college kid saw more than she should. *This is over*."

Emilio's dark eyebrows pinched. "You think so."

"You have Bianca," Nicola said. "Blood for blood. But this time, the blood's alive, and it will stay that way. She's a smart girl. She might not jump into your family business, but you have a live, healthy, eventually drug-free niece."

Emilio's gaze went to Jared. "A marker for a marker. Your girl for our girl, and our business is done. We want our man back."

"And that military rat as well," Boss Man offered. "We don't want him. You take him, or the cops get him."

Emilio rubbed the back of his neck. "Billy Tway. What a headache. Even with a babysitter, that man…yes. Both of them back. Is that our deal?"

"Affirmative," Jared agreed. "With all the Gianori family. Done. Forever."

Emilio nodded, agreeing with Jared. "Fine."

"Stay it to my face," Nicola demanded.

Surprise marred the mob boss's clean-cut Italian good looks.

Cash chuckled like an asshole, antagonizing the situation on Nicola's behalf. It made her smile on the inside, but outwardly, her gaze could laser cut a Mafioso's balls off. "Tell me."

His lip snarled. "Live blood for live blood. A Bianca for a Nicola. You're an unmarked woman, Mrs. Garrison. Feel free to breathe easy."

Fucker. She forced a snarling grin and, without a word, walked out the door, leaving the menfolk to go kill each other for all she cared. Not that a single Titan man would die that day.

———————————

"HANG TIGHT A SECOND." JARED veered off into a storefront as he and Cash ambled away from Vito's and their meeting with Gianori.

Still on an adrenaline rush and proud from seeing Nicola face off with a Mafioso asshole, he didn't notice as they entered the store and the world around them transformed. The lights were bright, the sounds were lyrical, and colors came from everywhere.

Cash shuffled to a stop in a...toy store. "What are we doing?"

Jared's face pinched. "Asal needs something. Whenever we're on the road in a civilized country, she gets a..." Boss Man gestured. "Thing. Book. Toy. Ribbon that goes in her hair. Stuff like that."

Cash knew he gaped but couldn't help it, and Jared didn't seem to notice or care but just went about his business. That big, bad motherfucker of a man was twirling a carousel of hair ribbons. "Holy hell," Cash whispered to himself.

But at the same time, he had an instantaneous pang. It wasn't jealousy. It was something else. Not a sense of parity—Asal was in grade school, and his child wasn't even born yet. But if Nicola weren't pregnant, would Jared have made this pit stop with Cash in tow? They'd worked together for years, and Cash had never known this was a thing.

"Dude, don't stand there with your eyes bugging out," Jared grumbled. "Someone's going to think you're a pervert, and I'll have to explain to Nic why you're in jail."

Okay...a boutique toy store. Not a big deal. He'd looked at baby-registry stuff with Nicola on a computer. This was going to be a something he did fairly often. But he still felt like a fake, as if he needed to prove that he was allowed to shop there. He needed to wear a sign that said: "It's okay. I'm allowed in here. I'm going to be a dad."

He *did* kind of have something like that in his

pocket. They'd gone for a sonogram, where everything was measured and Nicola was poked and prodded. Deciding against learning the baby's sex, they had a fallback plan, *just in case*, and that was in his back pocket—a sonogram and a note from the tech as to whether the baby was a boy or girl.

Until that moment, Cash had not been tempted to know. But now he saw thousands of fabulous things that one might buy a baby. Some were androgynous, but others were very feminine or masculine. His mind reeled.

Cash wandered the stacks of stuffed animals and trains, the ribbons and dresses, the make-believe world, and rows of bedtime books. He was awestruck. In the last five minutes, becoming a daddy had become even more real, and part of him wanted to run to wherever Nicola was and drag her back here to show her all the cool things.

He ran his fingers over a blanket, and the softness was unlike anything he'd ever felt.

"Can I help you, sir?"

Cash jumped, yanked out of his thoughts and ready to pull out the sonogram and prove he was allowed in there. "Just looking."

"It's our best baby blanket."

His baby deserved the best. "It's nice."

"Are you interested in it?"

Well, no shit; of course she'd ask that since he was

manhandling the shit out of it. "I'm here with a friend. The best?"

She nodded.

"My baby isn't here yet."

The woman beamed. "Congratulations. Boy or girl?"

A grin he couldn't stop formed. "We don't know."

"That's fun! When's your wife due?"

"January."

"Those come monogrammed. Do you have names picked?"

God, names. Should they have names picked out already? Were they so busy staying alive and recovering that he and Nicola had screwed up some unmentioned timeline—

"It's still early."

Cash took a deep breath.

"You're a first-time father?"

"That evident, huh?" He wasn't used to being read so easily. Showing his emotions was not his thing.

"Well, if you ever decide to get the blanket, you can call us, and we can mail it to you. How about that?"

His mind turned. No name. No gender. He needed something to surprise his sweet girl with. Nicola had earned it, and did they have, like, white blankets that were *the best*? Or the baby…a nickname… "What if…"

She waited.

The last few weeks of recovery from TBI had gone

well, but still, something was on the tip of his tongue, and it wouldn't come. Finally, his eyes closed. "I have the gender in an envelope." He reached for his wallet. "I want the blanket. Pink, blue, whichever. You look in here." He shoved the paper in her hand. "And whatever it says, do that. Don't tell me." Cash pinched his eyes closed, knowing that there was more. What was it? *God.* Like, on the tip of his tongue, something he wanted to say but couldn't. Then it came. He took a deep breath, relieved, knowing that it totally worked. "And no initials. Monogram *sweet one* on the blanket."

CHAPTER 19

"SERIOUSLY, HAS IT ALWAYS BEEN this cold in Virginia?" Nicola unwrapped the scarf from her neck. "I don't remember that."

"Maybe you're just thin-skinned."

She swatted Cash with the end of her scarf. "Hey."

"I meant, you literally have stretched yourself to the point that you are thin-skinned." He laughed.

"You're terrible!" She wrapped her arms around his frozen neck and kissed his equally chilled lips. "And you're cold."

"Warm me up, sweet girl."

"That's your line?" She kissed him again.

He laughed, unbuttoning her jacket for her. "I thought you and I were a sure thing."

"Handsome, I'm nearly nine months pregnant. Nothing's a sure thing"—she pretended to pull away from him—"except maybe a nap. I think I'll—"

Cash latched onto her neck, more making her laugh than turning her on. "You're awful! Oh my God! Cash, stop! I'm gonna pee!"

He erupted into laughter. "Hot, baby. Crazy, fuckin' hot."

Nicola rolled her eyes, still laughing, fortunately not peeing. When the baby might show up at any second, she wasn't joking all that much. "Whatever."

Cash dropped his jacket on the floor and pushed hers there too. Hand in hand, he led her to the living room, flipped the switch for the gas fireplace, and came at her with a predatory hunger she hadn't seen in weeks. It made her insides flip. "I'm not sure I'm up to whatever is going on in that devious mind of yours."

"I have a plan."

"I'll sink in the couch." Damn, there was that lazy-boy smile. Instantly, she was turned on just by the look because that smile said he wanted to dole out orgasms. That smile was a giving smile. It was great. "I might crush you if—"

"Sweet girl, shut your mouth if you're going to keep going like that." He cupped her cheeks and let his lips linger before he kissed her lightly. "Okay?"

"Okay."

"Let me play. It will be fun."

God…she thought about what happened when Cash played. "Whatever you say."

In the middle of the living room, he stripped her naked—big tummy, heavy breasts. If she could see her feet without obviously leaning and sticking out her leg, they'd be swollen. There was definitely a varicose vein or two. Or twelve. Whatever; she couldn't see them. Why count?

But wow—there was her husband, drinking in the sight of her naked, his erection jutting in his pants. "Cash?"

"I am so fucking lucky you are mine."

Every day, he took her breath away. "I love you."

He stripped off his shirt, nodding. "Love you too."

Nicola watched the mesmerizing action of him slowly unbuckling his belt, unsnapping his jeans, and kicking his shoes and clothes away.

The late-winter sun was fading the sky's light to a purple glow. It reflected off the snow in the great windows, casting him a perfect shadow as he came over and rested his hands on her biceps.

The simple action made shivers erupt all over her body. His mouth went to her neck, and his hands explored her breasts. Her clit begged for friction, and Nicola began to moan, sliding her thigh back and forth, shifting as she stood, wrapping her hands around his thick cock, and stroking him at a slow pace as he languidly kissed her body.

Cash kissed down her arm, sliding his tongue along the inside of her forearm, making her wet and needy.

He kissed the palm of one hand while his fingers intertwined with the other.

"That feels so good." She sighed.

He kissed pressure points, licking them, teasing them—just enough pressure, a little hard then so soft.

Nicola could've been floating as his fingers stroked between her legs. His thumb gently patted on her clit as his elbow widened her stance, and carefully, he opened her folds with a steady, rhythmic touch. "Easy, sweet girl."

Her arms hung loose, and her head dropped back.

"That's right where I want you." Cash guided her, and she was moving, but really, she was drifting, somehow walking, teetering on the edge of an earthquake-sized orgasm that was so damn gentle. With the fireplace right next to them, they stood in front of the large picture window and wood ledge, overlooking the purple-looking snow. Just them and God's country.

Cash came behind her, widening her legs by running his fingers along the inside of her thighs. "Good?"

"Yes." One half of her was cold, and the other felt the heat of the fire. Cash's strength and body enveloped her.

He positioned his erection against her waiting entrance, holding himself steady. His breath hitched. "Good still?"

She nodded. The intrusion was bliss. "Yes. Heaven."

Cash inched in, growling and taking his time. Nicola arched and moaned, having him pause and urging him on. There was so much pressure in the most excellent and overwhelming way. "Give me a second?"

"Of course." He rested his lips against the back of her neck.

"I need…something."

His tongue licked, and damn, she could feel that straight to her toes. Her vagina squeezed around his cock, and he shifted, groaning, maybe trying not to thrust.

"More, Cash." This was so good, but she just had to ease into it. Everything felt like too much, as if she could explode from orgasm or just combust.

He reached around and massaging her clit. Nicola hissed in approval, unable to even mumble thanks. Her hips flexed, and his did too, drawing out, just an inch, and thrusting in.

"Oh, that's amazing."

He sucked on her neck and thrust into her again. The rhythm was earth shattering. One second she was dying to come, the next minute, she thought she might die, no—wait. "OH, God."

The climax slammed through her—no prep time, no rising roll. Nicola arched her back and ground down on his shaft, panting and moaning and wanting more.

"Fuck, Nic."

It was intense but so short-lived. "More, please."

He worked her clit and took her from behind. Not hard, not deeper—just *more*. With his thumb flicking and cock strumming her, Nicola felt the incoming explosion again. She pushed onto her tiptoes, arching for him, leaning against the wooden half shelf in front of the window. Cash lay over her body, pumping into her.

"Give it to me," he ordered.

She nodded, wild and not caring, completely lost as he owned her body with every piston-like jacking of his hips. "Cash!"

He milked it, working her clit, riding her harder, faster. She blew through the fireworks, riding him back, gasping and praying that the ripple of muscles in her body would never stop because it was amazing.

She came again, feeling the heat of her husband's climax. They gasped, clinging to each other, needing that support and—"Ouch!"

He froze.

Giggling like a fool, she dropped her head. "I think I have a cramp."

Cash backed away from her, dropping kisses down her back. "A well-deserved one. That was a workout."

She stretched, and let him take her hand. "Shower?"

"Good plan."

Naked as a baby, Cash hit the kitchen for post-coital snacks, and they made their way to the master bath. He hit the steam shower, and she munched on the banana—*potassium,* Cash had said, for cramps—and nursed a bottle of water.

"Dang." She shifted on the side of the tub. "The banana's not doing it."

He gave her a look. *The look.* "Where's your phone? With the timer thingie."

"Nope." Nicola shook her head. "I have two weeks."

"Seriously?" He stomped off, still naked, and returned with her phone. "Where's it at?" He thumbed through her apps and held up one of questionable value related to man candy and gun porn.

"Book related, thank you very much."

He rolled his eyes. "Here. Set the timer."

"This baby will be on time."

"Oh my God," he said. "You've lost your mind."

"No. But I have a plan. I wrote it down, and that's how it will go. In two weeks." She smiled, suddenly knowing that she was having this baby very soon. Her stomach started to tighten. "*Shit.* Hit the timer."

Cash hit the button, and they both watched the clock.

"God, that's—" She shifted, this time ready for the discomfort. "A little sucky."

They did that, on and off, for the next twenty minutes and stared at the blinking results.

Time to go!
Time to go!
Time to go!

The bathroom was steamy with the forgotten shower. "I'm washing off for a second."

"We have to go!" Cash's voice was more urgent than she expected.

"We just *had sex*!" She stomped toward the shower. "Some things have to be cleaned up before I give birth."

He seemed to think that over for a moment before agreeing. "Fast."

Fast happened fast because a cramp—or rather a *contraction*—came upon her again. Nicola had her hair in a bun, and Cash had her dried off and in clothes before she could say, *Pass the granny panties, please.*

They arrived at the hospital after calling ahead and followed all the procedures they'd been trained to do. Easy peasy.

Nicola was checked in and given a bracelet and room before she could even call her family. Everything was efficient. That worked for her.

"Hi, my name is Anne. I'm going to be your nurse."

Nicola smiled as she was hooked to monitors. "I

had a birth plan. It was supposed to take place in two weeks."

"I'm going to be in Hawaii in two weeks, so that wouldn't work for me."

Cash laughed. "I like her."

"Yeah." Nicola ground her teeth as a contraction hit. "Me too." Who had time to BS about coulda, woulda, shoulda? "This baby is coming now."

"Let's see." Anne flipped on the machine. "Oh my. Maybe so." She ducked between Nicola's legs then popped back up. "I think you're right." With a big grin, she turned to Cash. "Dad, you ready?"

Anne moved to the wall, hit a button, and the rest became a blur. Something with a doctor Nicola didn't know, a no-bullshit nurse, and orders to push now and breathe. All Nicola knew was Cash held her hand like a champ and never looked away.

"Push, push, push!"

They gave her time to breathe. Nurse Anne didn't mess around and ran the room like the captain of a ship. Even without a birth plan, Nicola liked how in the midst of the first-babies-don't-come-this-fast chaos, there was order.

"Go, honey. Push, push, push!"

God! She *was* pushing! Her eyes were shut. Her world was dark. Nicola gave her body everything she had and—

A baby cried. Oh God! Their baby!

Nicola opened her eyes to see Cash's bewildered face. His eyes were wild, his mouth gaping, and he was smiling ear to ear, living and breathing pure joy.

"It's a boy!"

Things happened she couldn't see, and an overwhelming sense of accomplishment flooded her body.

"A boy," Nicola whispered. "We did it. My baby boy."

"Time to cut the cord, Dad."

With tears in his eyes, Cash looked at her and stepped to their little boy, seconds later reappearing by her side as Nurse Anne laid a semiblanketed baby on her breast. The baby instinctively moved his mouth to nurse.

Tears slipped down her face. "He's our sweet one, yeah?"

Cash rolled his lips into his mouth as though he choked on emotion. "Yeah, sweet girl. Our little man is a sweet one."

ABOUT THE AUTHOR

Cristin Harber is a *New York Times* and *USA Today* bestselling romance author. She writes romantic suspense, military romance, new adult, and contemporary romance. Readers voted her onto Amazon's Top Picks for Debut Romance Authors in 2013, and her debut Titan series was both a #1 romantic suspense and #1 military romance bestseller.

Join the newsletter!
Text TITAN to 66866
to sign up for exclusive emails.